UNDENIABLE

Also by Liz Bankes

Irresistible

UNDENIABLE

LIZ BANKES

BLOOMSBURY

NEW YORK LONDON OXFORD NEW DELHI SYDNEY

Originally published in Great Britain in 2013 by Piccadilly Press
First published in the United States of America in November 2015
by Bloomsbury Children's Books
www.bloomsbury.com

Bloomsbury is a registered trademark of Bloomsbury Publishing Plc

For information about permission to reproduce selections from this book, write to
Permissions, Bloomsbury Children's Books, 1385 Broadway, New York, New York 10018
Bloomsbury books may be purchased for business or promotional use. For information on
bulk purchases please contact Macmillan Corporate and Premium Sales Department at
specialmarkets@macmillan.com

Library of Congress Cataloging-in-Publication Data
Bankes, Liz.
Undeniable / by Liz Bankes.
pages   cm
Summary: Working for the summer as a runner on a television show filmed in London,
Gabi is surrounded by fascinating people, especially flirtatious Spencer Black, but when he
goes from extra to a featured role, it could mean another breakup for Gabi.
ISBN 978-0-8027-3623-9 (hardcover) • ISBN 978-0-8027-3624-6 (e-book)
[1. Television programs—Production and direction—Fiction. 2. Dating (Social customs)—
Fiction. 3. Celebrities—Fiction. 4. Summer employment—Fiction. 5. London (England)—
Fiction. 6. England—Fiction.] I. Title.
PZ7.B22555Und 2015   [Fic]—dc23   2014032449

Printed and bound in the U.S.A. by Thomson-Shore Inc., Dexter, Michigan
2 4 6 8 10 9 7 5 3 1

All papers used by Bloomsbury Publishing, Inc., are natural, recyclable products
made from wood grown in well-managed forests. The manufacturing processes
conform to the environmental regulations of the country of origin.

To Suzy,
who is always there with half-naked Ryan Gosling
and a wimple when I need her.
(Thank you.)

UNDENIABLE

CHAPTER 1

"Gabi," Julia says, looking up from her desk. "You wanted to see me?"

I always told Mia she was a loser when she said she used to be terrified of Julia. Mia hasn't worked at Radleigh Castle for a year, but she still shudders when I mention her old boss. Right from when I started working here I've said whatever I want to Julia, and she doesn't seem to mind; I've even made fun of her a few times to her face. She laughed once. Polly—one of the other waitresses, who follows me around a lot—says I'm brave. But I'm not feeling brave at the moment.

I really wish I had told Julia about this earlier. I kept meaning to, but then I'd find some reason to put it off because I'm worried she's going to say no. Two days ago I got as far as going to her office after my shift, but just as I got there Mia called me. When Julia opened the door I

1

chickened out and decided to pretend the phone call was urgent, so I ran off going, "OMG, I'll be there RIGHT AWAY! Just STAY CALM!" Mia was just calling to invite me to the movies. She didn't even think my reaction was that weird; she assumed I'd been helping myself to the chocolate truffles in the kitchens again. I had, but only a little.

Now I've gotten as far as sitting in Julia's office, and I am beginning to see what Mia meant. Oh well; the worst thing would be for her to say no. I take a deep breath.

"So I've got this thing," I tell her. "My granny called— she's an actress, but on stage, so not a famous one . . ."

I trail off, because someone at the window has caught my attention. Messy blond hair. Dressed like a bit of a prep—I mean, who wears button-downs in the daytime? Apart from teachers. And people with jobs. It can only be Jamie Elliot-Fox. He waves. I ignore him.

Julia frowns. "And . . . ?"

"Sorry!" I say, but I keep my eyes on the window. "And she knows this guy who is the father of this other guy who is the producer or something for *The Halls*."

Oh my God, he's kissing someone! The dick! Cheating on my best friend! I'll kill him. I will literally strangle— Oh no, wait, that *is* Mia. I'd forgotten she dyed her hair back to brown again.

Julia sees my eyes go wide and turns to look. Mia realizes they're by the window and pushes Jamie away, pretending to be really interested in something on the ground. Then she looks up as if she's only just seen us. She's such a fool. I wave at her, stopping when Julia turns back around.

2

"So he's the producer or something for *The Halls*," I continue, "which is obviously *am-a-zing*."

Julia shakes her head. "I haven't seen it."

"Oh my God, you should! It's *so* good. It's about all these students who go to college in London and lots of them get it on and some die and—"

"Gabi, can you get to the point?"

Okay. Here goes.

"Can I have the summer . . . off?"

CHAPTER 2

The train back to Granny's is absolutely packed, and I want to scream. I really don't understand how they do things in London. I thought that once the car was nicely full, people would stop getting on and wait patiently for the next train. NO. They kept cramming in, and I've ended up squashed in a corner with my face in a man's back.

I guess I should have expected it after catching the rush-hour train in this morning. I turned up all bright and cheery and determined to enjoy the commuting fun, despite the fact I'd had to get up at the crack of *death*—on summer vacation—and hadn't had time to wash my hair because I'd been wrestling my cretin of a sister for the last Pop-Tart. You would have thought she would let me have it, seeing as I was about to leave home and live in London for the entire summer. But she didn't. Because she is evil.

What I discovered on the morning train was that all

commuters are angry and silent. And that you have to be good at clambering when someone is sitting in an aisle seat and doesn't feel like budging up into the empty one next to them. The man I straddled did look a bit surprised, because I think he was worried I would sit on him at first. I tried to lighten the mood by telling him he had a nice newspaper (it's difficult to think of a compliment for someone with such an angry face) and by pointing out interesting things I saw on the trip (mostly birds and other trains), but all I got was a grunt. What a jerk. I probably shouldn't have said that out loud, though.

Just like then, as I now inhale this man's shirt, I am determined not to let it bother me. Today was the first day of my super-amazing, exciting summer, and nothing can dampen my mood. Especially not thinking about how I won't be spending the summer with my best friends. And definitely not thinking about the boyfriend I recently dumped. Or trying not to.

A few people get off at the next station, and I can actually breathe again. I've got a good spot holding on to a pole by the door. I feel a nice yawn coming on when suddenly the train lurches. This woman in front of me falls forward, and her whole fist goes into my mouth.

We stay like that for a moment, just staring at each other. And then she withdraws her hand, wipes it on her cardigan, and looks at me as though I were some weird person who'd tried to eat her.

I really hope no one from the production company saw that. I don't want to get a reputation for attacking people with my mouth.

I hear a stifled laughing sound and look over toward it. There's a guy leaning against the door a few feet away looking very amused. He's wearing one of those hats that sit on the back of your head—usually worn by arrogant people—and has dark curls of hair framing his face at the front. His eyebrows are arched kind of crookedly, and he has an irritatingly big grin on his face.

"It's rude to stare, you know," I say, and he just looks down at the book he's reading. Great; well, that's just made me look crazy.

Deep breath. Ignore dickheads. Focus on amazing summer, day one. To be honest, orientation today was not so amazing, and was mostly signing forms saying I wouldn't break anything or blame the company if I died while working for them. I was waiting for the part when they'd ask me which parts of the TV process I wanted to be involved in and I would say, "Oh, I'd like to be a scriptwriter and editor but, *you know*, if you *insist*, I'll also act in some scenes." And then I'd show them the writing I brought with me. But that didn't happen. Instead they said things like, "Make sure you're here early to put out the chairs for the read-through tomorrow."

I had tried to be early today, but ended up being only just on time because I got lost in Camden. Dad had printed off, like, seven maps for me, but on none of them had he told me which way was right side up. I was also dragging around a wheeled suitcase, which did not help. Neither does muttering "ass" and "balls" at regular intervals, but it does get people to move out of your way in case you are a lunatic.

I should maybe try that now, because the train is pulling into my stop, and I need to get to the door. The guy who was laughing at me earlier is in my way.

"Excuse me," I say in the firm and professional manner of a person with a job and not a person who gets lost a lot and attacks people with her mouth.

"All right, don't eat my hand . . . ," he mutters without looking up from his book. He steps to the side as the doors open.

I fix him with a withering glance (plus some hair flickage for good measure) and step off the train.

Into nothing.

Gabi: KILL ME.

Mia: What did you do?

Gabi: I fell into the gap between the platform and the train.

Mia: Of course you did . . . Are you all right??

Gabi: It wasn't actually very far down, and the gap was very big. And this guy picked me up right away. So it was fine, really.

Mia: I don't think I'd describe momentarily being under a train as "fine," but okay.

Gabi: So—other things that happened:

1. I met Johnny Green! Okay, well, I didn't technically speak to him. But we were in the SAME ROOM. Well, not at the same time. But he was in there just before me, and I GLIMPSED his HAIR. He left a coffee cup on the side, and when the guy was telling me about the job and all the important things I have to learn and remember, etc., I stole the cup and put it in my bag. Later I smelled it. I may have smelled Johnny Green! If I have, he smells like coffee. It could have been someone else's cup. Do you want me to send you a pic?

2. Have found out that being a runner may not involve actual running unless something "urgent" is happening, like pigeons invading the shot.

3. Someone's fist went into my mouth. But Granny made dinner, so I can't explain about that now.

I MISS YOU.

G x

Mia: I can't wait for your explanation for having a fist in your mouth. But I can live without seeing a picture of a coffee cup that smells like coffee and may/may not be Johnny Green's. Did you learn or remember anything that you will be doing on the job? I know you will ignore this, but don't be too stalker-y. How is it living in London? Things that have happened here in the boring countryside:

1. Nish said she saw a lion on the common. She went to alert the newspaper. Turns out it was one of those small, hairy ponies.

2. That is it. Nothing happens here. I CANNOT WAIT to go to France.

Please tell me more about your exciting London adventure or I will slip into a coma of boredom.

Miss you too. Lots.

Mia x

P.S. Jamie has already packed for France—he's taking his surfing shorts and a crate of wine, apparently. I told him it won't fit in his backpack.

CHAPTER 3

I was very lucky, really. I fell straight down onto the track and didn't hit anything on my way. Not even a boob, and I'm always hitting them on stuff. I once knocked a child over. Mia says I'm really lucky to have big boobs, but she doesn't realize that there's a lot of hassle involved. And backache. And people forgetting to look at my face.

I managed not to pull my suitcase down with me—it stayed balanced on the train step. My head was just above the platform. The laughing guy had gotten off the train and looked really freaked out. To him it must have looked like I just disappeared. At some point it finally occurred to me that I was almost under a train, which might not be the best place to stand, so I started frantically trying to clamber up. The guy put his hands under my armpits and heaved me up. I gave a rather unattractive grunt (not that I think there is an attractive version of a grunt). As he set me down on the platform, our eyes met. His were wide and sparkling, probably mostly with shock. My heart was thumping in my chest.

Then, before I could thank him, he leaped back onto the train just before it pulled away. I think he regretted laughing at me and felt he had to get involved.

I was left in a dazed state on the platform, and the other people around me looked pretty shocked as well. It was intense having lots of people watch me, so I said, "Well, I won't try that again!" Nobody laughed. They just looked away and carried on with their lives.

A station attendant came running over to me and fussed. He said that I should stay at the station until I recovered and someone could come and pick me up. I tried to explain that I was mainly just mortified and not actually hurt, *and* that I was staying at my granny's house about two minutes from the station, but he wouldn't listen. He said that my granny would be worried about me.

When she arrived she didn't seem very worried; she couldn't stop laughing.

"I wouldn't find it funny if you were gravely injured," she said. Which is good to know.

Mom made a bit more of a fuss when I called her on the way to Granny's. Although she also said, "But they make an announcement about that, don't they?" as if I'd fallen off the train because I hadn't listened to the warning telling me not to.

Granny moved to London after Grandpa died, and she has the coolest house ever. It's a converted church, and the room I'm staying in has an arched roof and a stained-glass window, and you get to it by going up a ladder. She's an actress, so there are posters from her plays all around and pictures of her with people who are probably famous but are from olden times, so I don't know them.

Also in my room is a photo of her and Grandpa. She's throwing her head back and laughing, and it looks like she's taking up the whole picture. Grandpa is a little blurry, and the sunlight is flashing off his glasses. He's kind of in the background, but I bet it was he who said whatever it was that cracked Granny up. She said that she could have gone off with any of these rich actor guys, but she knew Grandpa was the one for her. She would always say, "He looks like an egg with glasses, but he makes me laugh."

My sister, Millie, figures I was really "awful, insensitive, and frankly evil" at his funeral because I got drunk, insulted Uncle Nigel, and threw up everywhere. But I didn't mean to—the waiters kept filling up my glass. Besides, Granny found it hilarious. She said I livened it up, while everyone else was being boring and sobby. And I think it distracted her a bit from Dad not being there. Grandpa was his father, and he couldn't face it. And Uncle Nigel is a little grope-y. And only a tiny bit of vomit went into the cremation urn.

I lie back on the bed and stare at the beams. I should probably read over all the handouts I got today before I go to bed. Or I could lie here and picture tomorrow, when I'll get cast as Johnny Green's new love interest—on-screen and off.

I'll think about that.

And not Max.

CHAPTER 4

"Coffee." The man interrupts me when I am in the middle of introducing myself. He doesn't even look up from his desk.

"Oh, no, thanks," I say. Granny chucked two espressos down my throat this morning to wake me up.

He looks up now, but only with his eyes.

"The coffee run," he says wearily. "Kitchen's that way." He waves me away and snaps his fingers twice. He looks all bony and mean, like an angry skull. My face is burning as I turn away from him. I don't care if he's the producer; there's no need to be rude.

I leave his office and am tempted to pull the laminated card with his name off the door. It's not a real office if your name's just on a card, is it? If I had an office, I would have my name carved in stone.

Actually, it would probably be wood.

I head down the corridor. This place is huge. From outside it looks very old, with stone walls and high-up windows. It's right by the canal, so it sort of looks like a castle. Then when you get inside, the place seems even *bigger*. It's this mix of old and modern, with exposed brick walls, shiny wooden floors, and bright white walls. On the tour yesterday I saw lots of big rehearsal rooms, a studio rigged up to tape a game show, and plenty of production offices, editing suites, and makeup rooms.

There's this warehouse part at the back where they've put the set for the interiors of all the students' rooms. I immediately guessed which room belonged to which character; Nina, who was showing me around, seemed impressed, but not impressed enough to say I could have a souvenir prop to keep. But then I stole Johnny Green's coffee cup later, so it was fine.

When I get to the rehearsal room, all the actors are milling around the *very-well-put-out* tables and chairs that were my morning job. It's a big hall—the size of a school auditorium, but way cooler. The walls are all brick up to the big windows, and there's an arching roof with beams going across it. Definitely not like the auditorium at my old school, where the floor was all uneven and next to one of the radiators it smelled a little like garbage. And the chairs they have here are all black and stylish, as though they're from Ikea or somewhere.

We always used to complain at school that the chairs we had to take our exams on were splintery, and the pain distracted us from doing well. Then Mr. Garrick said in assembly that he'd had complaints that chairs were "pinching girls' bottoms," and they were forced to end the assembly because we couldn't stop laughing.

That just made me laugh now, and I accidentally snorted. Someone at the other end of the room has looked up and spotted me. A new celebrity friend, perhaps?

Oh my God, it's that guy from the train. What on actual earth is he doing here? He's grinning at me—because of the snort, I think—and then he mouths something that looks like "Hello." So I mouth "Hello" back. Then he mouths what he said again.

"Weirdo."

He grins, and for a moment there's a leap somewhere in my chest. But I narrow my eyes at him and then look down at my notepad as though I have far more important things to do. Like the coffee order. I cough, trying to get everyone's attention.

Nothing.

"HELLO!"

Well, that did it. They all turn to me, obviously expecting some important announcement.

"Who wants coffee?"

Of course everyone answers at once, and I don't hear anything. When I take orders at Radleigh Castle, everyone is well behaved and speaks one at a time. I try not to panic.

Someone nudges me. IT'S JEN. JEN FROM THE SHOW!

She's, like, the main girl and amazingly beautiful, but really mean. All of the other characters are scared of her, and she's the only one who can tame Harry, who's a total ladies' man, but unfortunately is also damn fine.

I'm a little scared that Jen has just nudged me. What if she makes me eat dog food like she did to that girl in season one? What if she hits me like she does tons of people?

She's smiling, though. And she doesn't look very hitty.

"Hey—you okay?" she asks.

I need to play this cool.

"YOU'RE JEN."

Cooler than that.

She laughs. "Ha, yeah. I'm also known as Bex. Who are you?"

"Gabi. I'm a runner. Would you like some coffee?"

She points at the pad I've been taking notes on. "Pass it around for everyone to write down their orders," she says confidentially. "Trust me, I did my fair share of coffee runs back in the day."

"Oh, thank you so much!" I smile at her, probably more crazily than gratefully, but she just shrugs.

"No prob. Good luck!"

I draw two columns on a page, write *Name* and *Coffee order* at the top, and hand the pad to the nearest person. My eyes go wide and I scream inside my head when I see that the person is Ben Hart, who plays Greg, the gay rugby guy. But other than that I don't react. I'm getting better at this. Ben smiles sweetly and says thank you. He starts the notebook going around the semicircle of tables.

While they're doing that, I don't have time to relax, because I also need to get everyone's scripts handed out. It is so very exciting seeing *The Halls: Season 2: Episode 1* written on them. I hope I get to hang around and hear the read-through. Most of the actors just mumble their thanks at me and then start flipping nervously through the script. There are a few new people, but I recognize pretty much everyone—even the really minor characters. It's so weird seeing them in real life, wearing track pants and tank tops and not looking all made-up and famous. It's like when you see teachers doing things like wearing jeans or eating chips. I get to the girl who plays Jas, who is really shy and geeky. Well, in the series she is, but then when the show started she did a photo shoot for a men's magazine where she whipped off her glasses (and clothes). She didn't seem so shy then.

Max printed out a picture of her from that magazine and stuck it on his notebook, and I accidentally tore it off. I don't see why she couldn't have kept her glasses on. I wear glasses for things like reading and looking at stuff. But I don't look like that naked. I'd love to steal her perfect ass. Maybe I should tell her?

I smile at her when I hand her the script, but she looks at me blankly and turns back to her conversation. I suppose I should stop assuming that famous people will recognize me just because I know who they are from TV, plus quite a few personal details about them from Internet stalking.

The next person I get to is the train guy who mouthed words at me. He's leaning against the wall by himself and reading a book again. And wearing the same hat. It's as though he *wants* to look pretentious.

"Are you one of the cast?" I say as if I totally don't care whether he is or isn't and as if I'm not thinking about his hands in my armpits.

I see a glint come into his eyes as he realizes who I am.

17

"Well, I have a line in here somewhere," he says, taking the script from me. Then I see he's holding the notepad with the coffee orders on it under his book. He holds it out to me and gives another wide grin.

The most annoying thing about it is that it makes me want to grin back at him. And I've got a fluttery feeling in my chest. I look away from him, because suddenly just the thought of liking someone has started a whirlpool of guilt and craziness.

"Thank you," I say, taking the pad and aiming to do my best strut as I walk off.

Then he calls after me, "Mind the gap!"

There's a janitor in the kitchen, so I read the orders while I wait to get to the hot water. You wouldn't think there could be so many different ways to order coffee. I don't know how I'm going to keep track of which cups have sweetener, no sugar, skim milk, regular milk.

The girl who plays Jas wrote *I'd love a hot chocolate with cream but I shouldn't lol.* And that is all she's written. So am I supposed to make her that?

Someone named Fred has written what looks like *Crrnnwap* so I'm not really sure what to do there either.

The last order on the list says *Spencer Black—Coffee, my place, tomorrow?*

Gabi has joined the conversation.

Gabi: Hello boys!
Mia: Hello!
Nish: LEAVER. You are dead to us now.
Rosie: He
Rosie: He
Gabi: What??
Rosie: I am in Nish's room and she keeps pressing
Rosie: enter
Rosie: when I
Rosie: try to typ
Mia: I'll smack her, just a min.
Nish: Good luck reaching me from your house!
Gabi: What's the goss, please?
Nish: You have left, Mia is going to France, nothing happens here, and Rosie and I are going to kill ourselves. Today I even looked through college applications—ugh.
Gabi: I've been hanging out with famous people.
Rosie: Sounds amazing :) Tell us all.
Gabi: Today was crazy! I had to get coffee for EVERYONE and then lunch for EVERYONE and photocopy all this stuff and straighten up all the rehearsal rooms and go out and find a stuffed mouse.
Gabi: So, the famous people:
The one who plays Jen seemed nice (unless it was a trick), Jas is not geeky in real life, Johnny Green is HOT. Gay Ben is ALSO HOT.
Rosie: Which one is Johnny Green?

Nish: He plays Harry! OMG. Rosie, your mom needs to get a TV. Tell her you're going to turn out weird and get bullied.

Mia: Can we rewind a second to "stuffed mouse"??

Gabi: It was a prop! So what have you all been up to while I've been photocopying and emptying the trash cans? (Correct answers are "nothing" and "missing you.")

Mia: Nothing. Missing you. Eating.

Nish: We went to a party. Mia kissed Jamie a lot. Many people tried to kiss Rosie.

Gabi: Still going well with the Foxmeister general, eh?

Gabi: ;)

Mia: Pipe down.

Rosie: No one tried to kiss me!

Nish: Saw Max there—ignored him, obvi.

Gabi: You don't have to ignore him. Was he okay?

Rosie: He seemed like he was doing really well, actually.

Gabi: Oh right.

Gabi: So I think you guys should visit me—EPIC NIGHT OUT! Except for Mia "I love going on vacation" Joseph. :(

Nish: This weekend?

Rosie: Let's reinstate Crazy Friday! I think my sister can lend us some of her friends' IDs for the night.

Gabi: YES!

Rosie: Imagine Crazy Friday in London—we might be able to go to a real club instead of having to make do with Spanky's!

Mia: Don't knock Spanky's—without it we would never have been able to see Gabi fall off a table into a trash can.

Gabi: I am glad you enjoyed it. I seem to remember that you all pretended not to know me!! Not as bad as Max, though, who recorded it and put it on YouTube like the lovely boyfriend he is.

Gabi: I mean was.

Gabi: I will see you guys on Friday, then. Au revoir, Mia—have fun being a frog!! Must run—Granny says dinner is ready! LOVE YOU ALL.

Mia: Pretty sure that's racist.

Gabi has left the conversation.

CHAPTER 5

So I've been best friends with Mia Joseph since birth, because we were born in the same hospital. Mia often points out that isn't "accurate" because we weren't born on the same day and didn't meet until later, but I say it's *symbolic* and because I sometimes forget.

We actually met in school, when we were five. Mia was really quiet and had an eye patch. I was obsessed with her and followed her everywhere. I've always really liked grumpy people. We sat next to each other in second grade. She never really spoke, but I used to make up for it by talking to her in class, nonstop. Then one day, when we had to draw pictures of our favorite animals, Victoria Fraser laughed at my picture of a cat, and Mia threw an apple at her head. She got into tons of trouble for sticking up for me, and her mom got called in. But she was going to be called in anyway, because Mia had drawn a picture of a shark eating a man. Anyway, shortly after that Mia asked to be moved because I was distracting her from her work. But I could tell she actually liked me.

We went to the same middle school and so went through our first kissing and boy-stalking experiences together. Not *actually* together, although quite often Mia would tell me and Max to stop making out when she was there because she was "trying to watch the movie" or it was making her "want to vomit."

When we were sixteen, we both left school to go to the junior college in the next town—Mia because there were all these electives she wanted to take, like photography; me because I sort of failed some of my exams. But I did get to take an events management class, and they are more flexible about me working at Radleigh than the high school would have been—although the teacher did notice when I fell asleep in class after I'd worked till closing time the night before. I thought I'd covered it up by wearing sunglasses, but then I snored.

In the first week of junior college we met Rosie and Nish. Rosie is beautiful, and boys always fall in love with her. She has a cool afro that on me would look ridiculous but on her looks all quirky and model-like. Nish is really fancy and was at private school until her parents split up and couldn't afford the tuition. She took a while to get used to the school, like when she asked us what house she was in and sat down in the cafeteria thinking someone would serve her. She's also friends with Jamie's ex, Cleo, which was a bit awkward for Mia at first. We've become a gang of four over the last year, though, and it's been awesome.

In terms of friends, I've had the best year ever. Other stuff, not so much.

"Cheer up—you look like a slapped ass," says Granny, ripping open a package of naan. When she says "Dinner is ready," she means "The takeout has arrived." I think Grandpa used to cook for her. She said she'd teach herself, but it's been a few months and she's managing to avoid it by going to restaurants and getting delivery. She tosses a piece of the naan at me. "How was your day?"

"Good! I put the chairs out and made coffee and wasn't too stalker-y around the famous people."

I feel a bit like I'm forcing myself to be cheerful. I had a really fun day, and yet all these glum feelings keep creeping into my brain. What's wrong with me?

Granny grins warmly. "Fantastic! You'll be doing something interesting in no time. It's a long slog, but do it with a smile."

I hear her voice change slightly. She must have noticed me staring at the table and not wolfing down my food like normal.

"You miss him?" She's leaning in to try to see my face, but I still don't look at her. Usually I'd be chatting away. I always spent hours on the phone with Granny, telling her all about any fights I'd had with Max or things that stressed me out at school.

But she doesn't question the silence. She leans back in her chair and breathes out a sympathetic sigh. "You're still allowed to be sad, even if you're the one who did the breaking up."

Just the tone of her voice feels like a hug.

Gabi: Are you still there, Mia? Are you asleep? If so, please wake up.

Mia: Hello! Yes. Still here and awake. Supposed to be packing. (Actually sitting next to empty suitcase while watching *Casablanca* again.)

Gabi: I'm having a sad moment. I look like this: :(

Gabi: You know movies have color in them now? You should try watching one.

Mia: What's up?

Gabi: How did Max seem to you?

Mia: It was hard to tell. He was being all outgoing and cheerful, but too much, I thought. Like he was putting on a show. How are you feeling about it all?

Gabi: I don't know. I miss him so much. But then I think I just don't want him to move on before I do. I don't want him to be depressed, just not happy without me! Am I awful?

Mia: No, you're normal. It's only been a month since you broke up! Do you want me to call you?

Gabi: Yes, please.

CHAPTER 6

I get up super early for my third day because I'm going to meet Mia and Jamie for coffee before they catch their train to Paris. It also means I'll be at work early, so I can have all the rooms looking lovely before everyone arrives. My enthusiasm lasts right until I get to King's Cross—so, about half an hour—and then my eyes start to droop. I am really not a morning person. If anyone says that they are, I get suspicious of them.

I'm waiting outside a café in St. Pancras Station. It's fancy and has a French name, so Jamie probably chose it.

It feels like the first time since I got here that I've had a moment to stop and think. I'm actually feeling really nervous about going to work. I think that's why I've been alternating between being manic and mopey. I'm always crazier when I'm nervous. When I have my shifts at Radleigh I never worry. I know exactly what I'm doing.

And Julia was always saying how impressed she was. She said it wouldn't be long before I could get a job as a wedding planner or something. That was really exciting—especially when I was imagining planning my own wedding with Max.

I feel a little stupid now.

"Hello." Jamie is standing in front of me, frowning as usual. His hair has grown out recently and he's got a beard. I'm going to have to warn Mia that he's letting himself go. Max grew a mustache for a bit last year because he said he felt comfortable enough that he could experiment and I would still love him. I told him that was absolutely true, but that I'd heard people saying he looked like a sex offender. It was only a small lie—when I said "I heard people saying," I meant "I thought."

"So you don't work for me anymore," says Jamie.

"I never worked for y— MIA!"

I run past Jamie and grab Mia in a big hug. Even though it's only been a few days since I saw her, there's a lot of high-pitched squealing. When we turn back, Jamie is wincing.

"I'll get the drinks."

He brings over some teas while Mia updates me on all the local gossip (very little) and I tell her more about my job. Jamie sits down and listens to our conversation for about a minute and then says he's going to try to find a wine list.

"There *will* be wine in France," Mia says, laughing a little.

"If I'm supposed to be getting on a train with members

27

of the public, then I'd prefer to be drunk," he mutters back.

"Are you planning on being a douche for the whole summer?" She's trying to make a stern face, but I can tell she wants to smile.

The corners of Jamie's mouth twitch into a grin. "I prefer you when you're angry, Joseph."

"Can you two stop being so happy, please?" I snap.

When they leave, and they think they're out of sight, Jamie puts his arm around Mia and kisses her on top of her head. I know it's stupid to be jealous, but everyone goes on and on about how great Mia and Jamie are together. Especially now that he's got his apartment—it makes them seem all grown-up. Everyone thought Max and I were silly kids when we said we were going to get married.

I miss being kissed.

"Don't you know it's rude to stare?" says a voice.

I look up in surprise. It's the train guy who has a line in the show. Spencer Black. With his stupid hat.

He's looking at me expectantly, perhaps because I didn't answer the note he left on the coffee order asking me out. They'd already started the read-through when I gave him his coffee, so there wasn't a chance to say anything then. But he glanced at me with crooked eyebrows, and I felt a jolt—which I quickly tried to forget, because that is really not what I want to be dealing with at the moment. He was hanging around at the end of the day, maybe trying to talk to me, but I barged past as though I had to leave really urgently because of something important.

I ended up going the wrong way and had to hide in the bathroom for a bit and come back out later.

When I realized he was behind me just now I felt the jolt again, as if the air buzzed between us. Something I definitely need to ignore.

"Going in early?" he says.

"Yes."

"Cool." He grins.

"How come *you're* going in early? Are you going to read your one line loads of times?"

He laughs. "No. I've been out. The club we went to was . . ." He stops to yawn massively. As he lifts his arms the bottom of his T-shirt rides up, and I can see the hairline on his stomach. ". . . open till seven, so I thought I'd go straight in."

He looks more stubbly than yesterday. I don't usually like the scruffy look. Mia always had lots of pictures on her wall of musicians she liked, and I called them her "band of druggies who don't wash." I always liked people who were clean-shaven and wore cologne and did their hair. But there's something pretty cool about the way Spencer probably just rolls out of bed in the morning. Or doesn't even go to bed.

"You take acting very seriously, then?"

"Well, as you pointed out, my part is very small."

I look at him for a second. His face is completely deadpan. Then we both start laughing. And I accidentally snort again.

He puts his arm around me. "Come on, runner. Let's get to work."

I shrug myself free. "Get off of me!"

But I can't help smiling. Or noticing that when his skin touched mine it made me shivery.

"Just being friendly," he says with a half smile as we head toward the entrance to the Underground.

"Or creepy," I reply.

As we go down the escalator he stands behind me and keeps making the Road Runner *meep meep* sound and making an innocent face when I look back. It reminds me of when Max would try to get my attention by poking me and saying "Hey," until I said "What?!" or—more often— hit him.

But at the same time it's completely different, because I don't know anything about Spencer. Maybe he always hits on girls on his way to work.

As we walk up from the station to the studio he tells me about his night. It sounds mostly full of drunken dancing. Then he says things got "sketchy" when his friend sat on a potted plant in this pretentious bar in Clapham. So I tell him about the time I fell into a trash can.

Apart from that, his life in London sounds about a million times more exciting than mine. He's been a student here for two years, and he's still finding new places to explore. He wants to live in London after he graduates, and I ask if he wants to be acting, but he says he only auditioned for a lark and for some "drinking money."

It's not a long trip, but it feels like we fit tons of talking in. He's really easy to talk to—not that I often find it difficult to talk, but he seems genuinely interested and doesn't stop listening, which some people do when I ramble on.

He doesn't mention the note he left me about going for coffee. It was obviously just a joke. Maybe we'll meet up as friends. It would be nice to have someone to chat with and to show me London. A London friend. As long as that's all it is.

CHAPTER 7

Johnny Green smiles and nods as I hand him a coffee and then looks down at his phone. There doesn't seem to be much potential for talking to him, which is a shame, because as well as being the hottest, he's also one of the few who is nearly the same age as the character he plays. Most of the cast are in their late twenties, but Johnny Green is just twenty. Spencer must be around that age too.

Johnny doesn't seem to be much like his character either. Harry is the main guy on the show and a total player. The scene where he went to meet Jen at the London Eye to take her on a real date and be her real boyfriend because he *really did love her* and didn't actually enjoy sleeping with lots of girls but she chose her boyfriend (Adam, with the squinty eyes) instead, and the last shot of the season was Harry looking sad with a glass of champagne—well, that cemented my love for him.

The Halls is seriously the best show ever. Season one was broadcast on Sunday nights, and on Monday mornings at school we would dissect every moment—like every single scene between Harry and Jen that had us screaming at the TV for them to just admit they loved each other, or the part where Greg told the rest of the rugby team he was gay and they all stood up for him against his horrible roommate who was bullying him—and when he started having an affair with his married tutor.

There's this couple on the show who had been together since they were at school—Priya and Tom. At first Max and I were like "That's us!" because we were going to live together while Max was at college. He got into the music school at Leeds, but we thought that was too far away, so he declined it and went to the college in town. I was going to work full-time at Radleigh and we'd get our own place, like Tom and Priya. Then they both cheated on each other and broke up.

I notice that the actors who play Tom and Priya are always sitting together and wonder whether they're a couple in real life. Or maybe they have lots of scenes together this season and will be getting back together . . .

A loud "Ugh" interrupts my thoughts. Heidi Adams, who plays Jas, just spat out a mouthful of coffee.

"This," she says, as if she's holding a cup of poo, "is *not* skim milk. I can't drink this."

"Well, you probably could if you tried," I say without thinking.

"Huh?" says Heidi, turning to look at me.

"Nothing!" I start rearranging mugs.

"Don't be such a diva." Bex, who plays Jen, leans over and holds out her drink. "Try mine."

"OMG, you are so rude!" Heidi hits Bex playfully and takes a sip. "Oh yeah, this is fine."

Bex winks at me. I trundle off with the cart that I persuaded my new friend Dave the janitor to give to me, slightly relieved, to the next person, who happens to be Spencer.

He half smiles at me. "So, you serve coffee with attitude."

"Shh!" I look around in case anyone heard him, but they're all engrossed in their own conversations. I think I'm safe. "Well, it's stupid," I say quietly. "Of course she can drink it. It's not like I peed in it. Although that's tempting for next time . . ."

Spencer laughs. "You still haven't responded to my proposal."

I freeze for a moment and look at him.

"We'll go for our own coffee. Coffee that *you* don't have to make," he says, "in some sort of coffee-making establishment—with baristas and sofas."

So maybe he wasn't joking. Am I being asked out? As in, on a date? With an actual man? This never happens to me. Well, it wouldn't, really, seeing as I've only ever had one boyfriend. But Spencer doesn't know that.

"Oh, no, thanks." It comes out automatically. I want to say yes, but somehow I can't. There's a guilty knot in my stomach.

He makes a pained expression and clutches his heart. "Cruel." He does actually look a little disappointed.

"I mean . . . I'm just . . . Well, you know, I don't feel . . .

I'm in London, and everything's new and weird, and I . . ." All the words are tumbling out of my mouth at a million miles an hour; I take a breath. "I'm really crazy at the moment," I say finally.

His eyebrows are raised and he looks surprised at my outburst. Then his expression softens into a smile. "Okay. Well, how's this: a strictly friendly coffee with your new London tour guide?" His eyes sparkle at me. "Nothing *untoward*—and you can be as crazy as you like."

I smile at him, relieved. And hoping we can both forget how I just freaked out.

My first date with Max was the lunch buffet at Pizza Hut. We'd met in the ninth-grade drama club, and it was in the days when he shaved off the sides of his hair and cut lines through his eyebrows because he wanted to look like a soccer player. But he was really funny. I got him to give me his number in case I ever needed an emergency drama partner and sent him some lighthearted texts (which took Mia hours to write), and then he asked me out.

He brought three friends along, and I brought Mia, Han, and Weird Laura from school. All the boys sat on one side of the table and the girls on the other. For the first five minutes everyone hid behind their menus and didn't speak. Except for me and Max. I didn't feel nervous at all talking to him. It felt like I already knew him. But at the same time, every sign that he liked me was like a jolt of electricity.

The other dates didn't go as well. Rob, sitting opposite Mia, was trying to impress her by talking about shoplifting candy from the newsstand. We would find out very soon that the one sitting opposite Han had the nickname Wandering Hands Pete. And Weird Laura stared at her date in silence until he made up an excuse and left early.

It went well for Max and me, though. Until I got a little overexcited and tried to order champagne and we had to leave.

CHAPTER 8

I wish I felt as relaxed and calm now as I did with Max. Or that I was still fourteen and it was socially acceptable to bring all my friends with me on a date. Not that this is a date. This is just a friendly drink with my London tour guide, who has nice curly hair and a bit of a beard. Which isn't my type. And attractive arms. I mean "attractive" in a friendly way.

I should have brought a list of witty, sophisticated things to say. With Max I just used to say things like, "I love your sexy butt." I never had to think about what I said. I suppose I could see if Rosie will text me some. She's good at knowing what to say—or at least she thinks about things before she says them and never blurts.

We left the studio and came into Camden. After Spencer had shown me around Camden Lock and the market, we ended up in a trendy coffee bar. Spencer says that his usual style is Lipton tea at home, but this is his first paid acting job, so he's celebrating by drinking outside of the house.

We are shown to a table, and the first thing I think is, *Those are really tall chairs.* I half consider asking him to give me a leg up, but instead put a foot on the lowest rung of the chair, make a move like I'm getting on a horse, and end up straddling the seat facing the wrong way.

"I'm sorry—I'm not very dainty," I explain, finding my balance and turning around.

"Well then, I don't think this is going to work." Spencer grins. "I'm incredibly dainty."

The fact he's said something slightly flirty gives me a leap of excitement. I always thought that all the uncertainty of not knowing whether someone liked me would drive me insane, but it also gives me a sort of thrill.

The coffee arrives, and the cups are absolutely tiny. The finger sandwiches aren't much better, and I think that calling them "toe sandwiches" would be more accurate. It takes us about a second to finish everything, and then we look at each other and laugh.

Spencer twists his mouth into an awkward expression, which I find sexy, even though I'm not supposed to be liking people due to being unstable.

"Shall we make this a coffee crawl?" he says.

The next place is a little Moroccan café down a side street. We lie back on low sofas that are really comfy and order honey and mint tea, which the waiter pours from a golden teapot that he holds really high in the air.

"I should try that when I get back to Radleigh," I say. We've been chatting easily the whole walk here and have covered my family, Spencer's film classes, and our jobs. Relationships haven't come up.

"A few people might get scalded until you get the hang of it," he says, turning his head to face me.

"I'll try it on the people I don't like first," I reply, meeting his eyes.

"Are there many?" He looks at me quizzically.

"Yeah, I have a list."

He laughs like that's a joke, but in fact I keep the list behind the bar.

He shifts around to face me on the sofa. He's telling me about all the things I should try to see while I'm here. He's so at ease, but at the same time you can tell how much he loves London. It sounds like every night out he has some random adventure that ends at a rave in a warehouse or getting invited onto someone's houseboat. His eyes stay steadily on me as he talks, and he leans in and gives me a friendly nudge at different points. Is he a touchy-feely person, or are these "moves"? It's like he's focusing completely on me. But that's what someone who's making moves would do, isn't it?

He's talking about how the pub next door has a really good comedy night that we should go to.

Without thinking I say, "Max went through a stage of wanting to be a stand-up comedian."

"Who's Max?" Spencer asks, his gaze still fixed on me. His expression is so open and friendly. He has no idea he's just asked a question that's started off a whole montage of sad thoughts in my brain.

"My boy . . . chum."

"Your boy chum?"

"Yeah, my boy chum from home. I have boy and girl chums. Do you?"

"Um, yes," he says, peering at me suspiciously.

It's probably because I hardly ever lie that I'm not very good at it. Usually the truth just slips out without me thinking about it. But I suddenly felt like I shouldn't tell him about Max, so instead I babbled at him about chums. I need Mia. She's good at being sneaky. She had a full-blown secret affair with Jamie last summer. Which obviously I've forgiven her for, but I do bring it up when I'm trying to get her to do stuff, like let me finish off a bag of gumdrops I found in her room or do my packing for London.

He gets a text and shifts around to get his phone out of his pocket. I take a deep breath and stare at the table, forcing the images of Max back into the dark little corner of my brain where they are supposed to stay hidden. Then I look over at Spencer, who's angled away from me texting.

He does have a nice butt.

Not that that's important. Nor is the fact that I can see a bit of tanned stomach at the top of his jeans, which looks quite sexy.

I should check my phone too in case there's anything from Granny. I texted her earlier to let her know I'd gone for a drink and would be a few hours late. She said, With a man? I said, Yeah, but not like that.

I find that she's replied Hoo. I think she meant to write Hmm. She texts with one finger while looking over the top of her glasses.

It reminds me of the time I gave her a lesson on

predictive text at Christmas. She was quite drunk and called it "protective dicks" by mistake and then cackled for about an hour. It makes me snort-laugh loudly into my tea.

Spencer puts his phone away and won't let me get away with not explaining.

"It won't be funny if I retell it!"

He leans over, so close that his curls brush against my forehead. "Come on! You can't giggle like a lunatic and not tell me why."

We both keep slipping into little laughing fits as I tell the story. He lies back again when I finish and laughs properly, but he's closer now, and our arms are touching. I can feel him shaking. When it finally subsides, we both turn our heads at the same time and look at each other.

I still can't get my breathing under control.

He walks me to the station and stops outside the entrance. "So," he says, holding his hands in the air. "First day with your guide. Are you pleased with the service?"

"Apart from the tiny cups," I say.

He nods. "I can only apologize. And promise you that next time the cups will be of an acceptable size."

A next time would be nice. Only in a strictly friendly tour guide way, obviously.

"Good. Well, I better go. Thanks for the tour."

I wait for him to move out of my way so I can go through the turnstile.

"Don't I get a good-bye hug?" He raises his eyebrows at me and holds his hands out. This feels more than strictly friendly.

"Um, okay. But keep your hands to yourself." I narrow my eyes at him and he laughs, which makes me smile.

We hug, and for a moment I am pressed against him. He smells good—sweet and fresh. A bit like apples, or something.

He moves back a bit and pauses. Our faces are inches apart. He turns his head slightly and arches one eyebrow. "Good-bye kiss?"

I swallow. It couldn't hurt to have a kiss, could it? It could just be a one-off, random thing. After all, I'm supposed to be single, and I can go around kissing people if I like.

But I don't feel like I'm single.

"You promised—nothing untoward!" I say.

I see his cheek twitch into a grin, and he moves away. "Ah, you can't blame a guy for trying."

CHAPTER 9

The next day I'm told I'll be sent to work with the location team to help finish getting the university buildings ready for filming over the weekend. This is *where it all happens.* Well, the scenes that are set on campus, anyway. They use the real student bar and club and some of the lecture halls, because they can shoot here during summer break. I'll be doing stuff like sweeping the floor, but at the same time I can scout out places where I might be able to accidentally wander into the shot.

When I'm sorting through all the paperwork they've given me—lists, props to check for, and these forms I have to go ask members of the public to sign if they end up getting filmed—Spencer appears at the door of the room I have started calling my office, but which is really just a closet I found.

He appeared just as I was singing to myself. I was singing the song from *Les Misérables* that's about hearing the people sing, but I flinch in surprise when I realize he's there and whack my head on a shelf. I don't think anyone has ever concluded that song by shouting "BALLS!" before.

I wait for him to stop laughing.

"So, Gabi, how does a party sound to you? I'm guessing you don't have many in your sleepy village."

I've told him I live in a pretty big town with its own nightclub and kebab shop, but he won't listen.

"We have lots of cool parties, actually," I say, not very convincingly.

"Are they in the church hall?"

"No!"

"Okay, well, I'll see you tomorrow, then. I'll text you my address. Drop by around nine?"

That does sound like fun. And it's the night Nish and Rosie are visiting. "My friends are coming up tomorrow."

He shrugs. "Bring them. You can all crash if you want; plenty of room in my bed." He gives a big grin, but for a moment our eyes meet and something flashes between us. A brief image.

They'll be so excited to go to a cool house party, but that image has made me feel funny about it, as if they might think I've gotten over Max too quickly and I'm chasing after some random guy. I can't even imagine being with someone else. Not for a second. That moment just now doesn't count. What's a good excuse?

"We can't. We have dinner plans."

"Do you go to bed immediately after dinner?" Spencer has an arched eyebrow and is leaning forward as if he's trying to win me over.

44

"Sometimes, when I've eaten a lot." It's true—once Max had to call a taxi to take me home from a noodle shop because I ate so much I thought I was going to slip into a coma.

He reaches over and pokes me on the arm with his finger. "Come on." He's looking at me through his curly hair. I'm burning all over, and at the same time I want to run away. Then he pokes me again. "I'll keep doing this until you agree to come to my party."

"Fine! If you're that desperate."

He smiles mischievously. It looks good on him. "Great, because I was thinking I really need someone to serve the drinks . . ."

CHAPTER 10

On the announcement board it just says *Delayed*. That's helpful. They were already held up getting into Waterloo Station, and then Rosie went all the way to the gate at London before she realized she'd lost Nish, who was waiting on the platform because she had assumed there were "people who take your bags for you." They got on the Underground, and last I heard from them they'd changed to the commuter train to get to Hampstead Heath. Maybe they've lost cell service.

Then the expected arrival changes to two minutes' time. I text them saying 2 minutes and they both reply separately with YES!

Two minutes later a train comes into view and the announcer lady makes her announcement, and I jump up and down a few times with a small squeal. A woman sitting on a bench gives me a weird look, as if to imply that I am a weirdo. I just assume that she isn't waiting for her *two best friends in the world* (apart from Mia) to visit her.

When I see Nish step off the train I run at her and scream. My scream is quickly joined by hers, and I'm sure even Rosie gives a faint yelp, but that could have been caused by my forceful hug. My run and scream make the woman on the bench jump. She makes a noise that sounds a bit like "Blap!" and hits herself in the face with her book. I feel a little bad, but not that bad.

After a session of hugging and jumping up and down, we finally start talking in words.

"So we are actually going to a party with famous people?" says Rosie.

"Well . . ." I consider. I may have exaggerated Spencer's party to make them more excited about the visit. "The guy whose party it is has a small part."

"Gross," says Nish.

"Oh dear," says Rosie.

"In the show, you perverts! But he's invited everyone. So all the cast could be there. Or none. Or some."

"I don't care," says Nish.

"We're here to see you!" says Rosie.

When we get back to her house, Granny has gotten out a fondue set and a whole bunch of fancy cheese that she says is from Borough Market. She's laid out pieces of French bread, grapes and carrots, and red wine and whiskey, which is for her, "because it's Friday," even though she drinks it every other day as well.

The mention of Friday leads into talking about Crazy

Friday, which obviously Granny wants to know all about. Luckily we stick to stories of me falling into a trash can, Nish ending up sleeping in a barn and being woken by pigs, and Rosie vomiting into a stranger's bag and not telling them. No mention is made of *anyone* mooning at the window of Pizza Hut.

Granny tells us all these stories about when she worked in the theater. There was this actor named Geoffrey who took himself really seriously and Granny and the other cast members played pranks on him, including Granny once bringing a pig onstage and then just continuing with her scene as normal.

Everyone is hooting with laughter, especially Granny, who has the loudest laugh known to man. Rosie says that we laugh in a really similar way. People are always saying how alike Granny and I are.

I can see what they mean. Granny says that her outspokenness skipped a generation in Dad, who is a worrier and what Granny calls a "sensitive soul," and went straight to me. Granny calls it "being forthright," but at school most teachers called it "not thinking before speaking." I think they spotted it my first week of high school when I told my tutor, Mr. Malone, that I was laughing at his bald spot instead of making up a lie.

Granny tells the story of how she met Grandpa. It's another one I've heard a million times, but I love it. Granny went on a cast outing to a bar in London to celebrate the opening night of her first play—she was a fairy in *A Midsummer Night's Dream*. Grandpa was dragged there by his friend, who offered to buy Granny a bottle of champagne in return for a dance. Granny saw a "short, odd-looking man standing there" and turned to ask him who he was. Before she could, Grandpa said, "Mine's a pint. You look like you can afford it." She turned down the dance with the friend and asked Grandpa if he'd like to dance instead, but he said he'd rather have a conversation.

"Big mistake," he said to me once. "Couldn't get her to shut up after that."

"And what we learn from that," says Granny, "is to always go for the one who makes you laugh."

We make our way steadily through the cheese. Rosie says something about not eating too much so we aren't bloated at the party, but I pretend not to hear her. She says stupid things from time to time.

Later, it turns out she may have had a point. When dinner is finished, the eating has made me sleepy, and I try to persuade them that going to bed now might be more fun than the party. They're not having any of it, and they drag me kicking and screaming—not literally (well, a bit; I do like to make a fuss)—back down to the station.

On the train Nish says, "Are all the places they go to on *Made in Chelsea* around here?"

Rosie says, "No, those are probably in Chelsea."

Because we had a bottle of wine with dinner, the conversation inevitably soon turns to penises.

"So," I say sadly, "I will most likely never see another penis again. I've decided to be celibate for five years. After that I'll be old so there probably won't be any point."

Nish raises an eyebrow, and Rosie says, "Don't be silly!"

"Surely they're all pretty much the same." Nish shrugs. She is going out with a girl named Effy and they've been together for two years, so she doesn't have much interest in penises.

"Are you forgetting about the *oblong* penis?" I remind her. That was a story involving Sandra from prep school, who is a few years older than us and shares a lot if you ever sit next to her in media studies.

"They differ wildly," says Rosie, and we start to nod along, before realizing what she's said and turning to look at her.

"WHAT?" I say.

"Wildly?" says Nish.

"Where have you seen these wild penises, Rosie?" I say, asking the question for both of us.

Rosie turns red and raises her voice above our cackling. "I just meant . . . everyone's different, aren't they? Anyway, what's this guy like? The one whose house we're going to."

"Fine! Just normal." I frown and fumble in my bag for my phone. When I find it and check the time I see there's a text from my sister, Millie, on there. I click to open it and see the word "Dad," and my stomach drops for a second. Surely nothing has happened; he'd seemed so much happier recently.

But when I read it properly, it says, Look at Dad's Facebook.

So I open Facebook and click on Dad's profile. He's apparently posted a status.

Gabi Morgan's body is covered in a thick coat of hair. It

has been difficult raising a wolf-child. Thank goodness my other daughter is normal.

I hate my sister.

I start to write a text to Spencer and get as far as `Hello` and then Nish, already giddy on wine, leans over and hits `SEND`. I give her a glare and write `Hello` again. Her hand darts over and again she sends the message. Now I have sent Spencer two messages just saying `Hello.` So I get Rosie to restrain her—she can do a sleeper hold; we're not sure where she learned it—while I start a new message.

`Hello there . . . Sorry my friend is`
`giddy on wine and sent those other`
`messages. We are on our way. Warning:`
`we are expecting hot actors (you don't`
`count) x`

We are chatting as the train pulls into Clapham and almost miss the stop. After a panicky leap through the closing doors we stand on the platform catching our breath. I feel my phone vibrate in my bag. He's replied already. Cool. That gives me a happy buzz.

`Don't think that was meant for me.`
`Glad you are having fun tho. M`

My heart drops. I sent the message to Max.

CHAPTER 11

A cheer goes up as we walk into Spencer's party, which brings me out of my guilt over texting Max. It's a three-story, old-looking house that he shares with five other people. As we go in, there are people chatting on the stairs and in the corridor. There's music pounding out of a doorway under the stairs, and a lot of noise coming from the living room. This is an actual, real party! Not like the ones we used to have at home, where we'd wait for Fat Steve to buy us beer and then end up dancing around to music playing from a laptop until someone (usually Rosie) threw up in their own hair.

The two guys who cheered us could be Spencer's housemates, although I don't think they know who we are, and they look a little like they would cheer anything. This is proved right when they cheer Rosie for hanging up her coat. They usher us in and introduce themselves as

Ravi and Sam. Ravi looks normal enough until I notice he's wearing a onesie, and Sam has a haircut that's shaved on the sides and long on top and wears massive black-rimmed glasses, which I don't think have any lenses in them.

We pass the doorway under the stairs where the music is thumping out, as well as strobe lights.

"That's the rave dungeon," says Sam casually, as though everyone has a rave dungeon under the stairs.

We weave around people in the living room. No celebrities, but Spencer still has lots of people at his party. *And* it's summer vacation!

Rosie and I make our way through to the kitchen, leaving Nish to figure out what to do with her expensive coat—she says it's well known that students can't afford nice clothes.

"So what's the deal with this Spencer person?" says Rosie.

At that moment the fridge door, which was open when we came in, swings shut to reveal a grinning face.

"Hello, hello." Spencer nods at me. "Thank you for the texts." Then he folds his arms and looks seriously at us. "So what *is* the deal with this Spencer person?"

I open my mouth to speak, but there are no words in my brain. "He's . . . ," I start.

Spencer waits, clearly enjoying every moment.

"He's a boy . . ."

"Chum?" says Spencer.

I nod.

"That's me," he says to Nish and Rosie. "Boy chum,

London tour guide, and provider of drinks." He gestures toward the fridge. "Help yourselves, ladies."

Spencer is a hit. Rosie thinks he's lovely, and Nish says he's "charming, for a boy." For some reason my first thought is that they never said anything like that about Max.

Max always made a big effort to get along with them. He burned all his episodes of *Game of Thrones* onto discs for Rosie after I told him how much she liked it.

I think I'm still feeling guilty about that text.

Nish went to find the bathroom, and we'd already lost Rosie to a crowd of excited men, so I'm left standing opposite Spencer. He's about to say something when some girls who have just arrived grab him. He hugs both of them and kisses them on the cheek. Then he's offering them drinks and asking them if they've missed him since the end of term. When one of them says no, he pokes her on the arm and says "Don't lie" and does his crooked-eyebrow thing.

He's obviously a massive flirt with everyone. I don't know why I've been getting so wound up.

I go to look for Nish to suggest some crazy dancing in the rave dungeon. I find her asking someone if there's a safe here, so I pop her coat into a nearby drawer and drag her down the steps.

Our hair-flipping creates a nice circle of space around us. I try not to, but I can't stop feeling a slight twinge of jealousy at the sight of Nish's perfect figure. Her body is amazing—boobs and butt all in proportion, even when she's throwing herself around like a madwoman and flinging her long black hair everywhere. Better than being all boob. That must be the first thing people notice when they look at me. It's why when I'm dancing I usually do something crazy, like jiggle them around or flash my bra, as though I'm saying, "Yes, I do realize I look ridiculous." And because it's funny.

In the middle of a get-low competition, which is no contest, really, with my low knees and Nish's long legs, Nish gives a look of surprise as her phone vibrates in her pocket. She pulls it out as we stand up. The name on the screen is *Effy*. Nish pauses and looks at me as if she's not sure whether she should go off to answer it or not, and I give her a shove toward the door.

"Don't you feel bad about being all happy and in love— it's my fault I'm not anymore," I tell her.

She fixes me with a look. "Now, we'll not have self-pity," she says, then throws her arm around my neck and gives me a squeeze and a kiss on the head. She's like that, Nish—all practical and sarcastic, but she always lets you know how much she cares.

I see her pass Spencer on the stairs, and she points over to me, probably telling him I need someone to dance with now. That's not strictly true, as I would happily dance on my own, but wondering whether he's going to come over gives me a thrill.

He's making a beeline for me, and when he reaches me he leans in so I'll hear him over the music. His stubbly cheek grazes the side of my face.

"I heard you're a crazy dancer."

My response, obviously, is to bust some moves. Spencer gives as good as he gets, and soon we're both going for it and keep cracking up as the dance moves get more and more ridiculous. I challenge him to a get-low competition as well, and it turns out he can get pretty low, despite being lanky. We end up with his knee between my legs and mine between his and at the same moment we both give way and end up on the floor, our legs tangled together.

We clumsily get to our feet, and when we stand up our bodies are pressed together as well. I can feel the thump of the bass vibrating through his chest. I see his Adam's apple move as he swallows and then he tilts his face around to mine. Our lips are almost touching.

The vibrations of sound are going right through my body, setting off an excited, tingly feeling. Then he moves toward me, decisively, and puts his hand behind my head.

"Wait," I swallow and nod over to the corner. It's in the shadow of the cellar stairs and completely out of sight. I move over there and he follows. I don't want to stop and think, just to be in the moment. I turn toward him with my back to the wall. He looks at me and grins, then he leans in. Our lips brush together, and as they do I pull his shirt, so he's pressing me into the wall. It feels all wild and new and uncertain, not knowing what it will be like to kiss someone else. And finally I kiss him.

It's like a note strikes off-key. I suddenly feel cold. The pulsing excitement that made me pull him closer has dissolved into fear, and I feel like I can't breathe. I twist my head away and push him backward. He takes a moment to realize what's going on and then drops his arms away from me, his eyes widened and confused.

I run around to the other side of the steps and then

lunge up them two at a time. In the hallway upstairs I barge past people to get to the front door, and then I'm out on the street. The chilly night air is a relief and I gulp it in, feeling space all around me. In the front window I think I see a couple of people looking out at me, so I walk over to a tree that hangs over the sidewalk and crouch behind it so I can't be seen.

I get my phone out and call Mia. There's a funny dial tone, and I remember that she's in France and hang up. I see Nish has sent me a text asking where I am, so I reply. She must have gone back down to the cellar after her phone call.

Almost immediately there's the sound of the front door opening and footsteps on the path. That was quick. I peer around the tree. But it's not Nish; it's Rosie. She comes out the gate and sits on the wall. She has her phone to her ear. I don't know who she'd be talking to at this time of night— although after her "wild penises" comment on the train I suspect she might have a secret boyfriend. I don't know why she'd want to keep it a secret, though. Unless he's weird. Or a criminal. I can't really imagine her going out with a criminal. When we tried to get her into a pub once it all got to be too much for her, and when the bartender came over to us, she shouted, "WE AREN'T SUPPOSED TO BE HERE."

Before I can go to her, the front door swings open again, and it's still not Nish—it's Spencer. He sees me and heads out through the gate. As he heads over, Rosie looks up and makes a panicky expression when she sees me. She tells the person on the phone she has to go and fumbles to hang up.

By this point Spencer is standing between us.

"Hey," he says, frowning. "Are you okay?"

I stare up at him, wishing I didn't have to explain.

"I told you I was crazy."

His eyebrows are raised, but he sounds amused. "Am I that bad a kisser?"

At that moment I catch Rosie's eye as she comes up behind him. She has a very different expression from the panicked one she had a few moments ago, but I can't really process it; my brain must be all over the place, because I thought the name disappearing from her phone screen was *Max*.

I swallow and look back to Spencer, standing there with his thumbs in his back pockets waiting for my explanation. He looks concerned, but he must just be wondering what the hell is wrong with me. I bet other girls he's kissed at parties don't freak out and run off. Kissing people is supposed to be fun.

In my head, I tell him everything: that I was with someone for three years, that I'd never kissed anybody except him, how it's all I know, and that all I could think about as we held each other under the stairs was how Spencer doesn't know me at all.

I thought Max would be the only person I kissed in my whole life.

Thinking that makes a big lump form in my throat that stops any words I want to say from passing my lips.

But just then the front door opens again, and Nish stomps out in her massive heels.

"Where have you been?" I shout, finding myself suddenly able to speak the moment I tear my gaze away from

Spencer. I can feel his eyes still fixed on me. Then I notice Nish has mud on her dress and a twig in her hair. "What have you been doing?"

"Running around the backyard in the pitch black."

That's a weird thing to do. Maybe she's drunk.

"Next time," she says, removing the twig, "can you be more specific than *I'm outside by a tree?*"

CHAPTER 12

I have a massive panic attack when I wake up at three a.m. in a random bed, before I remember that we crashed in one of Spencer's housemates' rooms. Granny said it was fine to stay as long as there were no men in the room. I texted her before we went to bed to let her know it was a man-free zone. She replied, `Lock the door—they sneak in.` I don't really want to know how she knows that.

Nish is sleeping facedown as usual. I am sure it's not normal and I don't know how she breathes, but Effy says she always does it. Tonight she has her arms by her sides, so it looks even weirder, as if she fell and knocked herself out. She also talks in her sleep, and apparently used to really freak everyone out at sleepovers. Once Nish texted me in her sleep in the middle of the night. It was really terrifying to wake up to a message saying `I can see you.`

I sit up in the bed and peer over to where Rosie is sleeping on an inflatable mattress. Her phone is poking out of the top of her bag. I could creep over and check to see if it *was* Max she was talking to, but that's a little crazy, even for me. It's just that the idea that there could be something going on between Max and Rosie has made me feel like I'm fourteen again and panicking over the thought that Max will like my prettier friends more than me.

But, at the same time, I *want* there to be something going on. At least it would mean that Max had done something wrong as well. Each other's friends are totally off-limits, even if I'm the one who ended it. If he'd gone there it wouldn't be all on me, the person who broke his heart and made him cry while I didn't cry at all.

The sad feeling swells up again. It's a cold sensation that makes me feel like my body is just an empty shell, because I hurt the person I was closest to. I swallow to force the sad feeling back down. My eyes hurt, but still I haven't cried. Everyone thinks I'm heartless.

The temptation to sneak a quick peek at Rosie's phone is too much. I just need to know. I slip out of the bed and creep forward, staring at Rosie despite only being able to half see her in the shadows, as if I will somehow read in her face what's going on. She moves her head—and her eyes open and look right at me. She's woken up, and seems terrified! To be fair, I must look pretty scary looming over her like this. I decide to make it look like I'm sleepwalking and slowly turn and walk back to my bed.

Now that I think about it, this probably looks even more frightening.

I lie on my side, closing my eyes but feeling all hot and panicky. What am I doing, being crazy toward Rosie? These guys were all here for me when I broke up with Max. When it happened Mia was spending the weekend in Wales with Jamie, and she made him drive her straight back. She brought around some Indian takeout and we sat in my room all day watching movies that had Ryan Gosling with his shirt off in them.

Mia let the others know, and when I got to school on Monday they'd made a Cheering-Up Gabi brunch, because they know I don't eat properly when I'm sad. Rosie had made cupcakes. She's the one who's good at hugs and saying lovely things. Nish gives practical advice like, "You should swear off men and be a lesbian." You wouldn't think we'd been a gang for only a year.

About an hour later I wake up again. It's four now, and I can still hear partying going on downstairs. I wonder if Spencer is still here. When Nish came out, I just ran over to her and didn't say anything to him. He called to me to wait, but I pretended not to hear.

I tried to tell Nish and Rosie that nothing was wrong, but they dragged me off and barricaded me in a bathroom, so I told them that I kissed Spencer and it made me feel sick.

Nish said that was to be expected. When she and Effy took a break, Nish hooked up with some girl at a party to make Effy jealous and apparently, when it came to it, she completely freaked out.

When she mentioned the jealous part, I caught Rosie's eye in the mirror and felt a squeeze in my chest because it made me think of her phone call. But I couldn't bring myself to ask her about it.

We vowed to go back out and enjoy the party, just the three of us, and went back down for more dancing.

Spencer was there, dancing with some girl. Maybe that's how it is for these college types—one girl freaks out and runs away, so they shrug and move on to the next one.

I kept looking over at them and may have accidentally given the girl the evil eye. Spencer saw me looking a couple of times and made a curious expression, as though he were trying to figure me out.

Lying here and absentmindedly stroking Nish's hair—it's very soft—I realize two things: one, Spencer was looking over at me too; and two, right now, I really need the bathroom.

I creep out onto the landing, praying that there is no one in the bathroom. If there is, I would actually have to go and do it outside—I'm that desperate. Spencer might not try to kiss me again if he found me peeing in his backyard.

"Hey," a voice calls through the banister by my feet, which makes me jump and (literally) almost wet myself.

Spencer comes up the stairs, also heading for the bathroom, but I nip in front of him to get to the door first. It's locked. Someone is in there.

"NO!" I'm bent over almost double and doing a little side-to-side dance.

Spencer looks at me with mock concern. "What's wrong?"

I give him a glare and a little jab in the ribs.

He shakes his head and then knocks loudly on the bathroom door. "Rav, get out."

There's the sound of some fumbling, then the door being unlocked. Ravi and some girl come out, looking disheveled and a little annoyed. I'm about to say "Get a room," but then I remember we're sleeping in Ravi's bedroom, so instead I just leg it past them and into the bathroom.

It is the best feeling ever. I am probably a bit too vocal about it, but I have honestly never been that relieved.

When I come out, Spencer is sitting on the stairs and gives me a weird look. I sit down next to him.

"Enjoying yourself?" He tilts his head toward me.

"That was the best and longest pee I've ever taken."

"You're really different from other girls I know, Gabi."

"I don't think I am. Anyone would have enjoyed that."

He smiles and then looks more serious. "Look, I'm sorry if I came on a bit strong."

He pauses, probably wondering whether I'm going to say something, but all the stuff about Max catches in my throat again and I stay silent—*highly* unusual. So he carries on.

"If I like someone, I just go for it. But I'd really like to keep getting to know you. I promise not to kiss you again."

"Good, 'cause it was really gross." I smile at him, grateful that he hasn't asked me to explain anything.

He nods. "Thanks for that."

"Do you want to stay here and chat?" I ask.

"Nah, that sounds terrible." He flashes me a grin, probably to avoid getting another jab in the ribs. Then he stands up and pulls me to my feet as well. "My room's a little more comfy. As long as you think you can keep your hands off me."

Spencer's room is right at the top of the house. It has a sloped roof and posters all over the walls—all of them advertising plays. Some of the plays are famous, like *God of Carnage* and some Shakespeare ones. But there are also flyers and pictures from college or high school productions, and a couple of them have Spencer's name on them. The poster for *Julius Caesar* has a picture of him in a toga. I lean in to get a closer look at that one.

He sees what I'm looking at and says, "What?"

A few things have surprised me. He actually is really serious about acting.

"You have a toned arm," I say, which was, in fact, my main thought as I looked at the poster.

"Do you want a good view?" he says.

"Of your arm?" I reply. That would be a little arrogant of him, not to mention weird.

"No," he says shortly. And then he climbs out the window.

CHAPTER 13

He's on a ledge, which is a relief.

There is a bay window below Spencer's room, jutting out from the front of the house and creating a wide ledge. It has a short stone wall running around it, but it still looks precarious. I'm leaning out the window with the curtain closed behind me.

"Come on." He pulls my hand. "What are you scared of?"

I look at him. "*Dying?*"

I am terrified of heights, which is totally logical. It's a bit like being scared of getting hit by a car or thrown into a fire. As I explained to Max while I was being lowered down from the treetop walk in Kew Gardens by the fire department, a fear of heights is far more rational than being scared of spiders, because heights are actually dangerous and can kill you. Although he just narrowed his eyes and replied, "The spiders in Australia can."

"I'll just stick my head out," I tell Spencer. Saves bothering the fire department.

"Fine," he says. "Wimp." And he leans back against the outside wall to my left. I lean against the window frame and look out at the view. All the streetlamps and car headlights are twinkling through the tops of the trees on the square. There's a light breeze whistling through the leaves above the murmur of people over toward the street—still out at four in the morning. These crazy Londoners.

We stand there just watching and listening for a few moments.

"It's like it's noisy and quiet at the same time," I say.

Spencer turns his head. "Deep."

I reach out to smack him on the head and he laughs. "No, I know what you mean."

And that's it. I find I can talk to him again, so we chat about the plays he's been in and how he loves the buzz of getting a line exactly right and feeling the reaction from the audience. It's stuff that Granny's told me about, so I tell him some of her stories. He says she sounds a bit like me.

He stands up and faces me. "You know, it's brilliant getting to talk about this. People think I just joke around all the time, but that's because it's easier than saying that there's something I really want."

"Because you might go for it and not get it, and then everyone would know," I say.

He nods. "Yeah." His eyes meet mine. They're serious and sparkly. "So what do you really want, Gabi?"

I shrug. "I'm just here to see famous people."

His eyes narrow. "That's not true."

Well, no, but it's embarrassing admitting that I have tons of writing ideas in a notebook. They're probably all stupid, anyway. I return his narrow-eyed look.

Spencer moves to climb back in the window. He puts his hand high up on the window frame to pull himself in, and his T-shirt rides up again so I can see some of his stomach. I step back to give him room, forgetting there's a curtain behind me, so we sort of collide.

"Well, this is awkward," he whispers.

I swallow. "Yeah."

He doesn't move, obviously thinking about my running away and freaking out, but I can hear him trying to steady his breathing.

But as he leans in I move my head a fraction. From this angle, the kiss would be on the lips. There's a pause. Nerves and excitement and just *wanting* are all pulsing through me.

He edges closer. Our lips are almost touching. And we pause for a moment. Just waiting on the brink. Something invisible is pulling me into him, and it takes all my effort to hold myself back. It's a leap into the unknown, just like before, and a ball of nerves and excitement flashes through me again, but this time I think the excitement is winning.

And then we both push together at the same time.

The tip of my tongue meets the tip of his. A feeling like fire is spreading through my chest and my legs and everywhere. And then he pulls away.

"Well, better get some sleep." His head is still inclined toward mine.

"Yeah, that's what I was thinking."

It was NOT.

He offers to sleep on the floor, but since it's a double bed I say that would be silly. Spencer agrees, as long as I don't grab him during the night. I tell him I'm not responsible for what I do in my sleep.

I'm turned toward the wall and grinning to myself as he slides under the covers. All this joking around, when beneath it there's the real possibility of something happening, is putting me on edge—in a good way.

On the wall next to his bed are a bunch of photos of him and his friends on nights out. In a lot of them he has his arms around girls and is grinning or pretending to kiss them. With Max, I knew all his friends, and he knew mine. Our social lives always involved each other, and I always knew where he was. Spencer's got a whole life that I know nothing about.

"So have you shared your bed with many men?" he says. It's as if he can read my mind.

I get that heart squeeze again. Imaginary Max pops into my head. All the times we were squashed up in my single bed. All the times we . . .

"Just one," I say.

"Really?" says Spencer, sounding surprised.

I immediately turn over on the pillow. "What are you saying?"

"No!" Spencer tries to dig himself out. "I just thought—you're all outgoing and confident. I thought you'd have lots of guys after you."

I thought I'd only sleep with one guy ever. And now I'll never be with Max like that again.

Well, that's your fault, says imaginary Max in my head. I wish imaginary Max wasn't such a smartass. And that he wasn't right. And that he wore clothes.

I look up at the photos on the wall again.

"Have you slept with lots of people?" I ask him.

"Ha! You're direct, aren't you?"

"Yeah," I say, still facing the wall.

"Okay, then. Twenty-four."

"Oh my God!" I spin around on the pillow and look at him again.

He's lying on his back, but he twists to face me. "It's not that many!"

"It is compared to one."

He pauses for a beat. I'm fiddling with the duvet. I know I've reached the point where I should stop talking. But I also know that I won't.

"Why does that matter?" Spencer shrugs.

Well, because if I sleep with you, you're way more experienced and I've only ever done it with one person, so I could have been doing it completely wrong the whole time and not even known.

I'm really glad I just thought that rather than saying it out loud.

Then I see Spencer's face and realize I *did* say it out loud.

"Not that I'm going to sleep with you, because things between us are strictly friendly," I say firmly and turn to face the wall again.

"Of course," he says, and kisses my shoulder.

CHAPTER 14

When we get back to Granny's the next morning, she's not there. It's a relief, to be honest, because out of everyone, Granny would probably be the one to notice that I seem different and have a bit of a happy glow going on. I snuck back into the other bedroom in the morning, and Nish and Rosie didn't even know that I'd left.

When they asked how I slept I heard myself telling them that it was fine, apart from Rosie's snoring. And that was it; I kept it a secret.

After I'd told them how the first kiss freaked me out, I didn't think I could explain the second one. And since it won't be happening again, they don't need to know.

"She went for a run," says Nish.

"What?" I call down from my ladder room as I change out of the clothes I wore at the party. "Why?"

"There's a note. She went with a friend," Rosie replies.

"How did she find another old person who likes run-ning? I didn't even know Granny liked running. Or had friends. She only moved here a few months ago. *I can't find my stupid sock!*"

"He doesn't look old," Nish calls up.

I stop looking for my sock and come over to the bal-cony, which overlooks the living room. They're looking out the window. I jump down the ladder and run over. Granny is waving at someone who I only glimpse as he disappears behind a hedge—there is a hedge between this house and the one next door; he's not hiding. I didn't see much, but I did see black curly hair, tanned skin, and a *tank top.*

Rosie smiles at me and I return it. I remember when she also brought cupcakes over to my house when my grandpa died. I wish she wasn't so nice. It makes me feel awful for suspecting her last night. And still now.

Granny sees us all lined up at the window as she turns back from the gate. She waves and grins at us, apparently not questioning what we are doing. The others scatter and look busy with breakfast as I open the door for her.

"Goodness! I am *shagged!*" she says, sitting on the sofa to untie her sneakers.

I feel my mouth drop open. The other two are trying to look interested in their mugs of tea, but Rosie snorts.

Soon we're all standing on the platform at Waterloo and getting ready to wave Nish and Rosie off.

They could have stayed another night, but Rosie has some family thing and Nish is going on some luxurious Istanbul trip with her dad and his girlfriend. Since

73

Nish's dad left her mom, he always takes her somewhere awesome, and she's allowed to bring Effy along, all expenses paid. It's balanced out by them having to hang out with her dad's girlfriend's evil twin twelve-year-old boys, Jupiter and Jacobi. When he took them to Florida, Nish was majorly annoyed when they didn't go to the Wizarding World of Harry Potter because the twins said it was a "stupid children's book."

I didn't tell her that I haven't technically read those books either—I listened to the audiobooks with Max, but I kept falling asleep and never found out who the monster was or where they hid the thing. It definitely would have been *much* better if her dad had just given her the money and she'd taken us instead, though he didn't agree when I told him that.

Granny and I hug them both, and I wish Nish luck on her trip. Rosie catches my eye as if she's going to say something, but then she doesn't and steps onto the train behind Nish.

We were watching one of my teen drama boxed sets, which Max was really scornful of when his friends were around, but which he secretly really loved. It was probably Dawson's Creek, which we got from Han's older sister—that was one of our faves.

I was supposed to be doing my English homework—a piece of creative writing—but every time the credits came up I kept saying "One more episode!" Mom, Dad, and Millie were out at parents' night anyway, so no one would check up on me. Then Max took control.

"Babe, I won't be allowed to stay here anymore if you don't do your work." He pushed my notepad toward me and handed me a pen.

I rolled my eyes. "Fine!" I went over to my laptop. "I'm just going to do some research . . ." I checked to make sure that Max couldn't see my screen and went to open up Facebook, but the browser was blank. "Hey!"

"I turned the router off," he said without even looking up. He was scribbling in his rap lyric book. "Can I call you Gaybie? I can't think of anything that rhymes with Gabi except scabby."

"Or stabby," I muttered darkly. "I don't even know what to write about."

He looked at me as if it were obvious. "Do something like Dawson's—like a couple or a love triangle or something."

"It's supposed to be literature-y. I'm supposed to use long words and write about death or describe some leaves in a way that's actually talking about death."

"Lots of literature is about love. Romeo and Juliet. Pride and Prejudice. The Notebook."

I definitely heard Max's voice break a bit when he said

The Notebook. *He cried for a whole hour more than I did when we watched it.*

He slid over to me on the sofa and put his arms around me. "Come on, babe. You've got tons of ideas."

So I started writing my story.

Before English class about a week later, Ms. Gregg came up to me. She said my story was "very funny and very real," and she was going to use it as one of the examples we would mark up as a class.

"OMFG!"

Ms. Gregg frowned at this.

"This has literally never happened to me, ever," I told her.

She smiled back at me then, but I could see lots of pink pen marks and comments (they don't write in red—it's too aggressive) on the pages she held.

"My spelling isn't great," I admitted.

She said that could be worked on so I didn't get marked down on the exam, and that the creative spark was the main thing.

But when she put my story on the projector and it was so big that it took up a whole wall of the classroom, all I could see were the pink pen marks.

"It's really hard to read with all the mistakes," said Tina, whose story had been the first one to go up—all perfectly spelled and about someone dying.

"It's huge. Maybe you need your eyes checked," said Mia.

"Maybe Gabi needs a special-needs test," muttered Tina, too quietly for Ms. Gregg to hear.

"On task, please!" said Ms. Gregg brightly, but you could tell it wasn't going the way she'd planned. She tried to get everyone to talk about the observational comedy and the message about

friendship—it was about a guy who tries to date two best friends, but when the friends find out they decide to humiliate him in front of everyone. But the whole way through, Tina and her squeaky little friend Melly (which isn't even a real name) kept pointing out all the mistakes.

Ms. Gregg tried to talk to me at the end, but I just left and didn't even take my story with me.

CHAPTER 15

When my alarm goes off at five in the morning, I briefly consider quitting my job, but then I have an exciting thought. Shooting starts today. I actually get to see some of *The Halls* being filmed.

And I'll see Spencer.

Which isn't important, because I've decided I won't be kissing him again.

Not that I was thinking of kissing him.

When I arrive at the university a load of white trailers is lined up along one side of the big park at the front of the campus. Some rooms inside the university building are used for storing props, but the makeup and dressing rooms and catering are all in the trailers. Except I got a text this morning to say that the hot water in the catering van isn't working, so I have to go find some big urn in the university cafeteria to use for making coffee.

The morning air is still really crisp. I walk around one of the makeup trailers and it's quite chilly in the shadow, but I come out the other side into soft, warming sunlight. Spencer is a few feet away, next to some people who are setting up a camera on a crane. He's talking to some girls on the crew, and their laughter keeps breaking out over the dull murmur of everything else. It seems like it's at a higher volume, and I keep looking over.

It's a good thing that he's hitting on other girls. If it was just me, that might make us a thing. And that could be the first step toward something big and scary.

As I'm telling myself that, I stop and watch Spencer talking. I feel as if I've only just started really looking at all the details of his face—the sharp angle of his cheeks when he smiles, the way his lips are always slightly parted.

All of which are irrelevant. I'm about to creep off in the other direction so he won't know I was here when he turns around and catches me staring.

"Hello, hello." He arches an eyebrow in amusement. It feels a bit like everything zooms into a close-up and we're the only two people here.

Then one of the cameramen says, "I said 'white, two sugars,'" and I accidentally shush him. I do a pretend sneeze to cover it up when I realize what he said.

"Yup," I say, and turn to the others for their coffee orders. My heart is pounding, and I wish I hadn't noticed Spencer's stupidly perfect jawline and how nicely his T-shirt fits. But I can't stop the buzz that goes through me when I see him.

I head into the university building to find the coffee urn, waving at people in the crew I've already gotten to know. The location manager, Nina, and her assistants are all really nice.

I take forever to find my pass in my bag, and the security guy—Ron—makes the joke he makes every morning, in which he pretends to not know who I am.

I'm in such a happy, skippy mood when I start making the coffee that I turn the knob with a bit too much enthusiasm and hot water spills out onto the floor. Just at that moment, Spencer appears at the door of the cafeteria.

"People are wondering where their coffee is— Whoa!"

He comes strolling in and is now looking at the massive puddle by his feet.

I look up from my search for a mop. "Do *not* tell anyone about this."

"Oh, don't worry, it's my fault. I must have startled you." He barely suppresses a grin.

But he starts making coffees from my list while I find a mop and clean up the water. It's possible I'm just sweeping it to the sides of the room, so we'll have to hope that no one hangs out by the wall.

Then someone else pops their head through the door.

"I think they pay people to do that, Spence."

It's Heidi, who plays the geeky Jas. She's wearing little shorts and suspenders with a band T-shirt and definitely looks cool, even though she's described as a misfit in her profile on the website. She's holding her glasses between her finger and thumb, looking intently at him.

All I can think is, *Why she is calling him Spence?* I'll Spence her.

"I've just been called," she continues. "Do you want to see my scene?"

He turns quickly toward her just as he puts a cup down, and the coffee spills over his fingers. "Sure!" he says, his voice catching slightly, as he must have scalded himself a little. He sucks the hot coffee off his fingers. "Are you all right here, Gabi?" His words are muffled by his hand.

"Oh yeah, fine!" I say, jamming my mop into the bucket a little too forcefully.

"Tell you what, I'll take some of the drinks out."

I smile my thanks, and as we catch each other's eye, it feels like the air crackles between us.

Heidi is inspecting her nails and breathes out impatiently.

"So I'll see you later?" he says to me, a smile still at the corners of his mouth.

I hand out the rest of the coffee and end up back at the makeup trailers in time to see the second scene of the day. About a million people touch up Johnny Green's hair before his first appearance, even though he's going to be riding a bike, so it will get messed up anyway. They're shooting the opening of episode two, because episode one is set during Christmas vacation and they all go off to Paris for New Year's. They're shooting that at the end of the summer after getting all the university scenes filmed. I won't get to go, since my internship will have finished by then, but I've already been to Paris.

Paris was awesome.

I yawn, then realize that one of the sound guys is watching me.

"You'll have to get used to this!" He laughs. He explains that because season two is set during the second term, which starts in January, all the outside scenes have to be shot really early in the morning so it doesn't look too sunny.

Harry's bike ride is filmed once by the camera on the crane, then with a camera next to him on a scooter, and then again with a camera fixed to his handlebars. It's so weird seeing him when they aren't shooting and he's just standing around with his arms folded, looking at his feet. Then, when the cameras roll, he's all full of energy and confidence and Harryness. The scene is supposed to be Harry racing to get to a hearing at the college where they're deciding whether to throw him out for plagiarizing one of his essays. He's turned into a total waster since Jen rejected him in the finale of season one.

Then after that, Jas finds him getting drunk after the hearing and offers to help him with the essay he has to write to avoid getting expelled. It's the start of a thing between them, which is going to be majorly controversial, because Jas is supposed to be best friends with Jen, Harry's ex, because Jen was there for her when her dad died and Jen showed she wasn't so mean after all. And because Jas is supposed to be all good and have morals and stuff. And you're just not supposed to go out with your friend's ex.

Even if the breakup was your friend's fault.

CHAPTER 16

When I walk through the door at the end of the day, Granny says, "You look knackered."

"I am! And I'm grumpy. I miss Mia," I say. "I wish she hadn't gone to France to farm grapes or whatever it is."

And I wish I could stop thinking about kissing Spencer in his room.

"Of course you do, love. Sit down and tell me. Have some sangria."

"Okay, thank— What?"

"Sangri*iii*a!" she trills. "And I made tapas. My running buddy, Alejandro, has inspired me."

I hope that's all he did to her.

She made the tapas only in the sense of taking things out of the packages and putting them into the oven, but it's still progress from takeout. It turns out that sangria tastes like cold mulled wine.

"I have something for you." She points at me and then rubs her hands with excitement. I hope it isn't anything weird. Granny's been getting weirder lately.

She comes out of her bedroom holding a little box and opens it to reveal a smaller blue box inside, fastened with a little gold clasp. Inside is a ring, with three tiny sapphires going across the top and two diamonds on either side of the middle sapphire.

I look up at her. "Are you asking me to marry you? Because I would say yes with this ring."

Granny laughs. "That's pretty much what I said when it was given to me. Charlie squirreled away money for months to get it. But I want to give it to you. And then one day, you can give it to your granddaughter."

I'm all choked up, as if there is a small rock sitting in my throat. I try to say thank you, but I can't get any words out. It feels like my throat is too closed up to speak. Then Granny makes it worse.

"I know this breakup is sad at the moment," she says, "but you're going to have so many adventures and meet plenty of new people who will understand how wonderful you are."

I try to say thank you again, but when my voice still doesn't work, I hug her.

Gabi has joined the conversation.

Gabi: Argh! So sorry I'm late, guys—work is crazy and my phone keeps freezing! What a nightmare!
Rosie: No worries.
Nish: Figuring out Rosie's birthday shenanigans—you need to get involved!
Gabi: YES. Ladies reunited!
Mia: Except me.
Gabi: That's what you get, froggy!
Rosie: So next Sat, out for pizza, then Spanky's?
Gabi: Uh. May. Zing. Just have to check my work dates. I'm dressing up as a giant condom next weekend. Argh, have to go now—they're shooting a bonfire scene where Harry plays Jas a song he wrote and they nearly kiss.
Mia: You're doing WHAT?
Gabi: Not supposed to tell you storylines. FORGET IT ALL.
Nish: Lol.
Gabi: Bye! xoxoxox

Gabi has left the conversation.

CHAPTER 17

The networking event is about a million floors up a huge tower. Apparently—according to my London tour guide—this is "the City." Large buildings loom over us, most of them made entirely out of windows, so you can see parties going on. Spencer points to the floor we're heading for. It looks very, very high up.

To distract myself in the elevator, I twist the ring around my finger. It's a bit too big for me, so I put it on my middle finger, but I might move it to my thumb. I would die if I lost it.

Spencer is looking annoyingly gorgeous in a shirt and nice pants, with slightly less messy hair than usual. He brushes it away from his eyes and fiddles with his collar.

"Well, this feels wrong." He wrinkles his nose.

"It was your idea!" I reply, hoping that he's changed his mind.

He's making out like I dragged him here. He was the one who spotted the poster for the Friday-evening television-industry event on a notice board in the Student Union. Then we talked about how awful the idea of networking was. He told me how Heidi Adams had told him he should "totally" go tonight, because he could "totally" get an agent and "totally" get some ad work. I told him that if he wanted to take the advice of a total idiot, that was up to him.

He thought it over for a moment. "We could go and laugh at people being dicks. And there's free food."

So here we are.

We haven't talked about the kiss. Or about sleeping in his bed.

I'm wearing my short green dress, jazzed up with my gold heels. It's a dress that keeps my boobs under control. They went a little wild the other day when I was wearing a tank top and had to run around to find some extras who had gone missing. One of the cameramen kept making comments about it.

I take a breath and try to look more awake. To be honest, the last thing I wanted to do was go out after spending all day doing things like making lots of half-eaten ramen noodles—so that a scene with Tom and Priya arguing while he eats them could be shot lots of times—and holding a branch out of a shot for *an hour*.

I e-mailed Mia to ask if she thought it would be a good idea to make up a fake name for the evening, but she said not to. I said it would be good in case I did anything awful so they'd be looking for someone else, but she pointed out that there would probably be people from my work there who would know me anyway. She does spoil my fun sometimes.

Granny said that the mingling and free drinks were all part of the fun. She put the emphasis on "free drinks."

Spencer turns to me as we go in the door. "So if it's awful, we leave?" He holds out his hand to make the bargain.

I go to shake it and then stop. "Not until after I've found the canapés."

He nods. "Deal." We shake on it, and his touch is electric-jolt time again.

As I scan the room, I realize that none of the other actors from *The Halls* are here. I suppose they've already made it and don't need to come to things like this. But I do spot the angry skull man who produces the show. His name is Colin, but I think Angry Skull suits him better. I'll definitely need to avoid him.

Looking out the windows is actually okay if you pretend that the view is just a picture and we're not really hundreds of feet in the air. It's amazing—miles and miles of twinkling lights.

Spencer swipes a couple of champagne glasses from a tray near the door and hands me one. In the meantime, a woman with a round face and a pointy nose approaches us. She tells us eagerly, and a little spittily, that we need to put on name tags and points us to a table with labels and pens on it. The temptation is too much. I look at Spencer.

"I have to do it," I tell him as I scribble my chosen name onto a label.

Spencer leans over to read it and laughs. "And who will I be?" he says.

I take another label. "You can be Storm, and your job is Clown."

It's hilarious watching people's eyes flick down to our name tags as they walk past us. So far we've mingled only with each other. The event isn't that busy, with it being summer break, and most people seem to be students. They must have come up specially for this, judging by their expressions of desperation as they search the room for anyone who might be important.

Then Spencer and I are approached by a girl who is wide-eyed and wearing a smile so big it must be hurting her face. Her name tag says "Helen," and underneath she's written "actress, writer, director, performance pot." I assume that's supposed to be "poet" but she ran out of room.

"Storm." She puts her hand on Spencer's chest as she reads his name tag. "That's a serious name for a clown."

"He's not very funny," I cut in.

"I aim to invert the idea of a clown by trying not to make people laugh, but to make them weep," Spencer says, completely deadpan.

She nods. "That's really interesting."

She gazes at him a bit too adoringly for my liking. So I chomp down on a cocktail weenie with deliberate force. She starts a little and turns to me.

"So you're . . . Cornelia Beard."

I nod.

"And you work as a 'fluffer.' What's that like?"

"Very stimulating," I say.

Spencer snorts into his drink.

"What exactly do you do?" says Helen, her smile slipping slightly, but still staying alarmingly big.

"I . . . Oh, I can't do it! It's a joke," I tell her. "I'm actually a runner."

"Oh," says Helen. The smile has dropped.

"Yeah, it's—"

But she's gone. Apparently being a runner isn't very impressive to a performance pot. I turn to the side to see that Spencer has been ambushed by a man in a suit. I sidle up and tune in to the conversation. Spencer has his arms crossed, covering his name tag.

They're talking about a filmmaker who is controversial, apparently, and they keep using the word "zeitgeist."

"Are you familiar with his work?" the man is saying.

"Oh yeah, yeah," says Spencer, "it's fascinating."

"And you?" the suit man asks me.

"No," I say. "What's it like?"

"The last piece was a silent short film of a performer, naked, with feathers and bells tied to his genitals. You watch as he slowly drowns in air. It was . . . incredible. Really encapsulated the circus of our lives."

"That sounds awful," I tell him.

Spencer's eyes go wide and the man jolts in surprise at me.

"I'm sorry," I add, "I didn't mean to be rude. It's just that I prefer stories with characters. And relationships. And words. And clothes."

"Your taste is clearly more for the commercial," says the man icily. He turns back to Spencer and they continue their discussion. Their conversation is so boring I want to poke my own eyes out.

I spot a friendly looking waitress with a tray of canapés and make my escape. I chat to Anya, the waitress, for a while and she lets me have three mini beef Wellingtons. She tells me about her husband and son in Poland and that she only sees them every six months. I feel silly remembering the time Max and I said we couldn't possibly go to different colleges and only see each other every couple of weeks. I tell her that I am supposed to be networking in order to start my wonderful career in television, but I am not very good at it. She says not to worry, as she has waitressed at lots of these things and most of the people are mentally deficient.

I look over at Spencer again, and now he's talking to a sharp-looking woman with a severe bob haircut. He's gotten rid of his name tag. I wonder if I should go over and instigate our get-out plan of tapping him on the shoulder and saying, "We have to be there at eight, you know," as if we're off to some other important event. I realize I may only be thinking of doing that because he looks so engrossed in conversation with the woman. Then Anya gives me a nudge.

Angry Skull is making a beeline for me. There's a lurch in my stomach as I remember my name tag, so I cover it with my hand, even though it looks a lot like I'm holding my boob.

"Hello, Gabi."

"Hi, Angry—hiangry . . . *Hungry*. Are you . . . hungry?"

His skull eyes narrow. "No." He's twirling a cocktail stick in his fingers, a little like he might stab me with it. "I've been hearing good things about you."

"Oh, I . . . What?"

"Yes. Nina, the location manager, is a fan. She says you're well organized and gave them a lot of help getting the set ready."

"I made friends with a tall man with a ladder," I tell him to prove it.

"What's your endgame?" He is pointing the cocktail stick at me now.

That's not an easy question. I have no idea what he wants to hear.

"Um, I don't know. I just like being here, really." That's probably not very impressive, but it's true. "I like being involved with something that entertains people and makes them happy."

"And what is it that you like so much about it?"

"Oh my God, just *everything*. It's those couples that everyone loves so much that they make up names for them, you know, like Tiya or HarJen or Mabi. Except not that last one. Or characters you like so much you make a montage of topless pictures of them and upload it to YouTube."

He's about to reply, but I'm on a roll. May as well get it all out now.

"Or knowing that sometimes the best part of a story line is something absolutely *heartbreaking* happening, because if you're really devastated by it, then you know you must really care. You know, like when Jas's dad died."

I pause. I think I'm done. Oh no, there's more.

"Or it's the way that the most uplifting moments are timed perfectly, like the part where Greg's rugby team walks into the bar to back him up against that bully, and everyone was like *yes!* It would be amazing knowing you were making that stuff happen."

He looks a little startled. I probably got carried away. I hadn't really thought about all that stuff until I said it. I mean, obviously I was super excited to come and do the internship when Granny mentioned it, working on my absolute favorite TV show, but a lot of it was wanting to get away. Mia was going to be in France. I would have been at Radleigh full-time for the summer, and I was sick of everyone whispering behind my back and then giving me pitying looks while they told me how well I was doing. I wanted to escape, really, and be somewhere where no one knew me. But now that I'm here, I'm actually thinking that this could be something I'd be good at.

"I might be able to find you some more interesting things to do," he says finally.

My eyes go wide as I look at him. Maybe I can ask to meet some of the writers? I could bring my story ideas with me and show them and just tell them to ignore the spelling.

"Do you think I could—" I start.

I feel a tap on my shoulder.

"We need to be there by eight, you know," says Spencer.

CHAPTER 18

I feel uneasy about leaving so quickly. But Angry Skull did say he would see me tomorrow, so hopefully he meant what he said about the interesting things. It probably would have been better to talk to him more, but I had about a millionth of a second to decide. It was clear Spencer was leaving, and I didn't really want to be in a room of weird people by myself. Also, it was what Spencer and I had agreed on.

As I am thinking that and we're walking out of the lobby of the building, I look over at him, and he looks back quizzically with his crooked eyebrows. A happy buzz goes through me.

"Who was that woman?" My voice comes out a little singsong. I think I'm a bit high on the fact that Spencer has left a party to hang out with me. And possibly a bit tipsy from the champagne. I should calm down.

"She's an—"

"Great!" Oops, I reacted too soon.

"—agent for lots of reality TV stars," he says, fiddling with his screwed-up name tag. "People who are famous for doing nothing. Completely opposite to why I want to go into acting."

"What was she saying?"

"Some crap about my look being 'hot and edgy and now' and that she could get me lots of advertisements or something."

"Oh my God! Are you going to do it?"

"Nah." He laughs. "Anyway, let's go have an adventure."

I text Granny and say that the networking evening is dragging on. I thought that was probably better than saying I was wandering the streets of London.

The road we go down is completely deserted, with big, old-fashioned stone buildings on either side and lit-up skyscrapers rising behind them. It's so quiet, Spencer says, because all the bankers are inside making their money, even this late in the evening. Then we arrive at a huge intersection. There's another old building with pillars at the front that looks like a temple, and we take the steps down to Monument underground station.

Coming out at Embankment station, we walk up a busy pedestrian street along the side of Charing Cross. Spencer takes out his phone and checks the time.

"Still open," he says.

I look at him questioningly, but he's not giving anything away.

He leads us past the station and toward Trafalgar Square. I notice he's untucked his shirt and rolled the sleeves up.

The fountains look cool, sparkling in the lights as the sky starts to darken into evening.

"Are we going to the gallery thing?" I ask.

"Nearly," is all he tells me.

We veer to the right of the main National Gallery building toward an entrance that definitely looks familiar. As we go in and head up an escalator, I realize that Granny and Grandpa took us here when we went inside the National Gallery. It's the one with all the portraits of the kings and queens. I really liked it, but Millie kept making fun of me for being a geek, so I kicked her right by the portrait of Queen Elizabeth and we got escorted out.

"Oh my God, I love this place!" My voice comes out really loud and echoes a lot. The people in front of us on the escalator turn around and glare, but Spencer just laughs.

"ME TOO!" he shouts.

He says there's an exhibition going on, so we skip past the main galleries, which is a shame, because I remember liking the portraits and wondering what the people were like in real life and who they had affairs with.

The exhibition Spencer wants to see is called Behind the Scenes, and it's photos of actors in rehearsal or right before they go onstage.

We're there forever as he spots his favorite actors or photos from plays he's seen. Some of them I recognize (the ones who've been in the Harry Potter films, but Spencer doesn't sound very impressed when I say that) and some of the older ones Granny has told me about, like Laurence Olivier, who apparently was "bloody gorgeous" in real life.

We come back out into Trafalgar Square when the gallery closes and sit up on the side of the fountain for a while, looking back at the gallery building. It's dark now and the building is lit up, making it look even more massive.

Spencer is talking about how we should go see some theater and how he's really annoyed with himself that he hasn't been for a long time. I love the way he frowns and gestures with his hands while he's talking, as though he really cares about it. He's much more interesting than when he's saying things about zeitgeists and people with feathers on their genitals.

Spencer jumps down and grabs my hand and pulls me down too. "Let's go out."

My heart lurches.

"You mean like boyfriend and girlfriend?"

He's still holding my hand, but his eyes have gone wide. "Um, I meant to a bar."

"Oh, I thought so." I try to sound casual, but it comes out all squeaky.

He raises an eyebrow. "Did you?"

"No."

"Brilliant."

He's got a very amused expression as we head away from Trafalgar Square and toward Soho. I drop his hand and fold my arms and keep telling him to shut up, even though he's not actually saying anything, just looking at me in a really annoying way.

My heart is thumping against my rib cage. As certain as I am that I don't want to be someone's girlfriend, at this moment all I want is for him to kiss me.

We go to a bar where some of Spencer's housemates are; it's next to a place where I think I spot some actual naked women. Spencer tells me to stop ogling, but I reply that I'm not ogling, just curious. You don't get much nudity back home, except sometimes at the outdoor swimming pool, but that's usually accidental.

There's Ravi and his brother Ajay, and Sam with his girlfriend, who's also named Sam and who also wears big glasses that might not have glass in them. They're all ordering shots, and because I'm hanging out with a bunch of twenty-year-olds with beards (except for girl Sam), I don't get asked for ID.

I only remember to call Granny and tell her I'm staying at Spencer's when we are inside the bar and I can't really hear her properly. I'm sure it's fine, though—Granny's really laid back and knows how it is. She moved to London when she was eighteen.

Spencer's friends seem impressed with my crazy dancing. We dance as a group, but I'm always close to Spencer, and we keep brushing against each other. I catch his eye, and it's like there's a charge between us, an unspoken, uncertain thing that's pulling at my chest.

Max and I had our first time all planned out. It was going to be perfect. My parents and sister were away. I had made my bedroom look all nice with candles and the nearest I could get to rose petals (feathers from the boa I wore at my sixteenth birthday party). Mia and I had been on a highly secret mission to the supermarket to buy condoms and Milk Duds. The Milk Duds didn't have anything to do with it—we just didn't want to only be buying condoms—although I did wonder whether they might be useful for regaining our strength afterward. When I said that to Max, he looked worried and told me not to expect too much.

Almost as soon as my family left, Max (who had been hiding behind a tree) was at the door. I opened it nervously.

There he was, holding a stuffed pig. He looked more nervous than me, even though he'd sort of done it before with his previous girlfriend, Fiona, who I don't like.

"I had a little time to kill, so I went to the arcade and won you a pig," he said.

I grabbed him by the T-shirt and pulled him toward me. From that moment I wasn't nervous at all. I wanted him as close to me as possible. Our lips met, and we were kissing against the wall in the hallway. His hands were tangled in my hair, and mine were running over his chest. I traced my fingers down over his stomach until they reached his belt. And we stopped. His forehead was on mine. The pig had fallen to the floor.

"Shall we go up to my room?" I whispered, trying to keep my voice level.

"Yep!" He laughed, breathing as quickly as me.

I led him up. His hand felt warm. My heart leaped at the thought that this was all happening with the person I liked best.

We got to my room, and had enough time to do some kissing and for Max to say "Why are there feathers on your bed?" when the doorbell rang.

My aunt Jill had stopped by to see how I was getting on, and I had to hide Max in a closet. Some of the feathers had stuck to him, so if she'd found him, it could have looked really weird.

CHAPTER 19

Back at Spencer's house the drinking continues, and I really don't think I can keep up. I also keep breaking the drinking rules by using forbidden words such as "drink" and "the" and so have to down some of my mug—they didn't have any wineglasses—as a punishment.

Spencer sits over on the other side of the room from me. I'm sure I catch him looking over a couple of times. When our eyes do meet, it feels like the air crackles between us, and I'm sure it's not just me.

When we need a new drinking game I suggest Articulate, because I've played it at Mia's a bunch of times and am a total pro. But they don't have it. Sam (boy) suggests Trivial Pursuit, and Sam (girl) says she's really good at it. My heart sinks.

When we play that at Mia's house I always make sure I pair up with her brother, Matthew, because he is freakishly smart and knows where all the countries are. But he's not here now. Maybe I could secretly text him? I don't have his number, though. And he probably doesn't have a phone because he's only ten.

Spencer and I are a team, and it's awful. We only get pie pieces because of him. Obviously that's what happens when I'm on a team with Matthew too, but Mia's family wouldn't care if I thought Beirut was a kind of vegetable or if I got some centuries mixed up. Some of the questions that the other teams get—like the name of Charles II's most famous girlfriend—I definitely do know. But when I say I knew it was Nell Gwyn, no one looks like they believe me. I have a book of royal scandals that Granny gave me, and Nell's was one of my favorite stories. She was just someone who sold oranges (and maybe did a little prostituting), and she ended up going out with the king. Maybe if I get a box of apples and stand outside Buckingham Palace, I could end up going out with Prince Harry.

Sam (girl) says that they don't teach dates in history class at school anymore and shakes her head, which is really annoying, as she can't have left school that long ago.

"History is just one damn thing after another," says Spencer, and he gives me a friendly shoulder bump. I want to hug him for rescuing me, but he undoes it when a question about Greek gods comes up and he says, "You should know this—aren't you Greek?"

Sam (boy) pipes up, "Oh! I thought you looked a bit . . . you know." And he points to my face.

"Foreign?" Ajay grins, and then Sam turns bright red.

"Oh, no, no I didn't . . ."

But Ajay slaps him on the back and tells him he was joking. It's a bit like when Dad first met Nish and asked her where she was from. Nish told him she lived down the road, and Dad said, "Oh no, I meant where are you from originally?"

Nish said, "Luton."

"So you're Greek?" says Sam (girl). "It's such a fascinating place. I've always thought ancient Greece was a culture dominated by a prevalence of dichotomies."

I stare at her for a moment. I'm sure some of those words aren't even real. "My granny's Greek," I say. "So I'm only a little. The only things I know about Greece are from watching *Mamma Mia!*"

She gives me a pitying look. I probably know a bit more than that, but I want her to stop asking me history questions. And to shut up.

"I think," says Spencer, "what would be *really* interesting is a game of I Have Never. I'll go first. I have never fallen into the gap between the platform and the train."

He grins at me. I smile at him, do a little salute, and take my drink.

The whole room lurches.

This is much more fun, especially since Sam (girl) is much more open than Sam (boy) about their relationship and keeps embarrassing him. I probably let on a bit too much about myself.

I catch Spencer's eye a few times. He drinks for quite a few things. It's weird not knowing someone's past. Around his friends, Spencer seems like he just spends all his time partying. You wouldn't know he took anything seriously.

And they keep talking about his "moves" and all the girls he's been with. He laughs along with most of it, but a couple of times I see his eyes dart over to me, as though he's checking for my reaction. I throw myself into the game and just laugh at the things they say about Spencer as well. But underneath it all, I wonder.

I suppose at college it's not really a big deal, which is weird, because at home whether a couple is going to do it is something that gets talked about forever and planned and you have to go through the whole rigmarole of finding a bed, or bush (Nish), to do it in.

The funniest part of the game is the way Ajay and Ravi go after each other because they each have so much dirt on each other. "I have *never*," says Ajay, looking right at Ravi with a gleam in his eye, "farted in front of the whole school while playing the recorder and then run out of assembly crying."

Ravi narrows his eyes and glares at Ajay as he drinks.

"*I* have never been *engaged*," he says.

Ajay takes a swig. "Man, that's a low blow," he says, laughing but sounding a litttle annoyed.

And then everyone looks at me. Because I just drank.

I was trying to pack for New Zealand. It wasn't going very well, because Mia kept taking stuff out of my suitcase and saying things like, "You can't take that much makeup" and "Where on the bus are you planning to plug in your hair straightener?"

It was her fault I was going on this vacation of danger and most likely death. I had been planning to make out a will, but Mia said I would probably have to go somewhere and sign things, rather than just fill in something on the Internet like I thought, so in the end I dropped the idea. I sent Max a text saying that when I died I was leaving everything to him, and I wrote GABI MORGAN at the end so it would be like a signature. I told Mia she was my witness, and she agreed. Well, she said, "Hurry up and pack!" but she did nod slightly while she said it.

Then my sister, who had been listening outside, put her head in the door and asked if she could have my clothes, because Max wouldn't need them. So I said, "You haven't seen him on Thursday nights," and she ran off saying she was going to be sick. Max does look surprisingly good in a bikini.

Eventually I shoved all my stuff into a backpack (and snuck my makeup back in when Mia was in the bathroom—and my heels) and we were ready. Jamie was going to give us a lift to the airport in his fancy car, and he phoned to say he would be there in half an hour. I made Mia put him on speakerphone so I could ask him if he was excited about the playlist I'd made for the trip, entitled It's Gabi, Bitch. He said, "No," so I told him that would only make me sing louder.

There was a tap on the door, and Max's head appeared.

"MAXIE!" I was about to leap on him, but he interrupted me.

"Um, can I speak to Mia for a moment?"

I eyed him suspiciously. "Okay, as long as you're not having a steamy affair." I think I saw Mia try not to laugh. So I went out of the room and left them alone. Obviously I listened at the door. Max was giving Mia something for me to open on Christmas day. I smiled to myself at the thought of the stocking I'd given his mom earlier.

I went back into the room to give Max his good-bye kiss, but it went on a little longer than I planned and Mia went and waited downstairs because she felt uncomfortable.

On Christmas day we were with my cousin in Auckland, enjoying the hot tub. We Skyped our families, and then I did Skype stocking opening with Max. I told Mia she could be there too if she wanted, but she said we might do something gross. After she'd gone into another room I realized she'd left a wrapped-up shoe box next to me.

When Max appeared on the screen I held the box up.

"Oh my God, you got me some shoes!"

He froze.

"Max?" Then I realized it was the screen that had frozen and he was talking.

"Ummm . . . just wait."

He started moving again and opened his presents first. I got him a Jay-Z album, a PlayStation game, and a hat to replace the one that got ruined in Paris.

"Thank you, baby!" He leaned over and kissed the camera.

"I'm sorry it's not the same as your old hat—they'd sold out!" They hadn't; this hat was just much nicer.

"Your turn," he said. He looked really nervous.

I tore open the wrapping paper and lifted the lid. Inside was a lot of shredded tissue paper. And a stone.

"Um, thanks?"

"No! That was just to make it heavy."

I'd thought Mia looked grumpy dragging her backpack around.

"Oh!" *I chucked the stone away and started digging around in the tissue paper. And found a little red box.*

I looked up at the screen, and Max was holding up a piece of paper:

MARRY ME?

CHAPTER 20

"Joking! Obvi," I say. They look at me as if I'm weird. Spencer is peering at me as though he's trying to tell if I really am joking. "Unless you count the drunk man who proposed to me outside the grocery store," I say quickly. "He did say I was a beautiful lad. And he'd wet himself."

Everyone laughs and turns to Sam (boy) for the next one. Spencer keeps looking at me for a second longer than the others.

I'm having trouble focusing, and I feel like I might fall over, even though I'm sitting down. I also want to move on from the engagement moment quickly, so I turn to Spencer and politely ask him to remind me where the bathroom is. Well, that's what I say in my head. It comes out of my mouth as, "Can you take me for a pee?"

I don't think I really appreciated last time the fact that their bathroom is absolutely massive. I wait until I hear

Spencer get to the bottom of the stairs and go back into the living room. Then I sit on the toilet, get my phone out, and call Mia.

It's really lucky that I do actually call *her* and not someone random, because I'm just sort of jabbing the phone with my hand.

While I'm dialing, a text message from Nish comes through. I see it has the word "tomorrow" in it, but that's all I catch before I accidentally delete it.

"Hello?" Mia says in a little faraway voice, like a tiny mouse. Then she says it again because I haven't actually answered.

"Heyyy," I say.

"You're drunk," she replies immediately.

"You sound crackly!" I'm whispering and holding my hand over my mouth, even though I'm sure they won't hear me from down in the living room.

"I'm in France . . . Where are you? Oh, Jamie says hi."

"Tell Jamie I hate him. He's stolen you off. Away. I want you back."

There's some rustling, and then Jamie's voice comes on the line.

"She's yours for ten pounds. I've been looking to trade her in."

Then I hear a "Hey" and a scuffle, and Mia's back on. "So where are you?"

"Just at Spencer's." I'm trying to sound casual, but my throat is too tight.

"Is that the guy who had the party?" she says. "The others told me about him."

"What did they say?" I've stopped whispering, but my voice is still coming out higher than I mean it to.

"That he kissed you and it freaked you out. Gabi, what's wrong?"

"Wrong? Nothing! How are you?" I swallow.

There's a pause and some shuffling. It sounds as though she's moving to another room.

"Gabi," she says firmly. "What would you be saying if this was me?"

"Come to my bosom and tell me everything," I mumble.

"Exactly," she says. "So, you know . . . do that."

Mia doesn't like naming body parts.

So I tell her. About the kiss and how I can't get it out of my mind. About all the things his friends were saying about him just now. How I look at him and have no idea what he's thinking, but I get a thrill every time I find out something new about him. How exciting it is being at the point where everything is a possibility. And how scary. And how the idea of trusting someone fills me with panic. Mia just listens and lets me speak.

"I don't understand how it happened." I catch my breath. "I got scared, and I'm drunk, and now I've run away to hide in this *huge* bathroom."

"What do you mean?"

"Well, it's just massive. You could run around and around the room to dry yourself instead of using a towel."

"No—what do you mean, you don't understand how it happened?" she says.

"I think I like him."

"It's okay to like him," Mia says softly.

I pause. "No it's not! I only just broke up with Max. People will think I'm heartless."

"Anyone that matters knows you're not heartless, Gabi. If someone thinks otherwise, they're a moron."

"You won't tell anyone, will you?"

"Well, this is awkward, because I've been live-tweeting our conversation."

"Oh Mia, even in France you're still a jackass."

"'Fraid so."

"But you're my jackass."

"Um, thanks. Do you think you'll tell him you like him?"

"No. He might not even feel the same. And if he does, then he shouldn't get involved with me anyway. I'm crazy and all over the place and shouldn't be allowed near people."

"You are very crazy, but you're also amazing and I have the highest standards in the world for anyone who goes near *you*. He would be lucky to be involved with you."

"I love it when you're sappy, Mia."

"Shut up."

I smile and then lean my head against the toilet paper holder and neither of us says anything for a while. It's one of those comfortable silences that you can have with your best friend. I close my eyes.

"Gabi? GABI?" Mia's voice is barking at me. "Have you fallen asleep?"

"Sorry!" My eyes snap back open.

"You should probably go back downstairs now. You've been on the phone with me for about half an hour. They'll think you're throwing up."

I stride back into the room and say, "I wasn't throwing up."

They all look up at me. Now they definitely think I was.

Spencer stands up—all three of him, in fact. He looks concerned, I think.

"Shall we take you to bed?"

The time it did happen with Max probably sounds cooler than it was. It was in a car at a house party. But the car was his older brother, Cal's, and the party was Cal's friend's, so we didn't really know anyone there. Mia and some of the other girls from school were huddled in a corner mostly saying "What?" and repeating themselves a lot because the music was so loud. Mia was actually hoping to get with this guy Kieran (who I now call Kieran the Dick) but I didn't know that at the time, because Mia is all sneaky and secretive with stuff like that. I beat it out of her in the end. Not literally. Well, a bit literally.

They weren't being very partyish, so I dragged Max around to mingle, but that backfired because he started talking to some guy about soccer and didn't seem to notice all the yawning and eye-rolling I was doing. Eventually I said, "Max! I think someone is starting a beat-boxing competition!" and he went, "Ooh, where?" and I took him off to the kitchen.

I went behind Max and threaded my arms under his and squeezed him. I was in one of those moods where my heart just buzzed with how much I loved him.

"Let's get drinks!" I said, while Max was looking around for people beat-boxing.

It was a huge kitchen, which blatantly contained everything you could ever need, so we set about finding the ingredients for Jaegerbombs.

"One, two, three—drink!" said Max.

I was busy making my disgusted shots face before I realized Max was looking at something.

"What?" I turned around.

"Those are Cal's car keys."

I turned back. The question was there in his eyes.

Outside it was chilly, and we both had our arms crossed to try to stop the shivering. We hadn't stopped to get our coats. Looking back at the house, we could see the silhouettes of people through the curtains. We didn't think anyone had seen us leave. Both our heads turned in panic to the house again when Max pressed the button to unlock the car, causing a loud beep and the headlights to light up, but nothing changed.

Then once we'd slid into the backseat, Max decided to try to put the front seats down to make it more like a bed. He pushed the one on the driver's side too forcefully, and the headrest smacked against the horn. We both squealed—him more high-pitched than me, I think—and then we were silent. But again the house didn't react.

The seats were freezing, and at first our kissing was disrupted by frequent shivering. I moved on top of him, and he hugged me close. I went in for a long, slow kiss and slid my hand over his chest and down. He moaned slightly as I felt him straining against his jeans. He shifted over, and then we awkwardly repositioned ourselves so I was lying back on the seat and he was lying on his side on the front seats.

"Clothes off?" he said.

"Can we keep top halves on?" I asked.

"Won't that look weird?"

"Only if you go back into the house like that."

He flung his jeans away in an impression of a stripper before realizing that the condom was in his pocket. Then I couldn't stop laughing at his butt in the air as he scrambled around to pick them up again.

Then he was on top of me, our bare legs together. He moved a strand of hair away from my face.

"I love you."

I smiled at him. "I know. Get on with it."

When it actually happened, it was like everything went quiet. There was nothing except the sound of our breathing—and whispering, because he was worried about hurting me and I was telling him it was okay. I can't remember exactly what we said. It's all a blur. But a happy blur. With Max I felt completely safe.

Afterward we lay there hugging for a while, but we knew we couldn't be long. Cal was supposed to be giving us all a lift home, and they would be wondering where we were.

We found out that actually they weren't. We'd been seen going toward the car and word had gotten around to everyone except Mia, who had left her lip gloss in the car and had come out to get it. A minute later, she'd run back into the house shouting, "MY EYES!"

CHAPTER 21

I'm sitting on Spencer's bed. He left me to get changed into a T-shirt.

I could tell him how I feel—that I like him. It could start something. Something that would take over and throw us together and send us on an adventure.

Something beyond my control.

He puts his head in the door and holds up a toothbrush. "Spare," he says.

"Do you keep one handy for all the girls you bring back here?" I shoot back. It comes out more angry than I meant it to.

"What's it to you? I'm just your tour guide," he says. He says it in a jokey way, but there's an edge to his voice.

"Who said I cared?" I look up at him defiantly.

He frowns. The room suddenly feels tense and awkward. But there's no going back now. He sits down next to me on

116

the bed. "I see what's happened here." His voice is low and serious. "You lurve me," he says.

It takes me a moment to process that.

"What?"

"You really lurve me, don't you?" His voice is all husky.

"No, I don't!"

"You do!" His eyes are all wide, and he's pouting.

"I do not." I jab him in the ribs.

"Ow! Look," he says, "you wanted this to be strictly friendly. So I've been behaving myself." A smile creeps in at the corners of his mouth. "Mostly."

The moment crackles in the air between us, and I smile at him.

"But for the record," he carries on, "I think you're hilarious. I don't know why you're so fixed on this 'friends' thing, but if that's something you can't tell me, then that's cool. The main thing is, I like hanging out with you. I'd like to keep hanging out with you."

I get the urge to grab him and kiss him and start off on whatever adventure will happen if I do. But I can't just yet. Also, the room is still spinning, and if I let go of the bed, I might fall over.

"How do I know these aren't lines you use on all the girls?" I say.

He shrugs. "You'll just have to trust me."

I pad back into the massive bathroom, following Spencer and holding the spare toothbrush.

"You know, you could just run around and around in here to dry yourself. You wouldn't need a towel," I say as I make my way to the sink.

"That's what all the girls say," he says dryly. "Actually, no. No one has said that before."

We both look at each other and then start brushing our teeth at the same time. I am surprisingly coordinated, seeing as I was having trouble sitting up. Then I catch Spencer's eye in the mirror. Involuntarily, we both break into grins. Which causes me to briefly drool, so I quickly move my face over the sink. When I look up, Spencer is still smiling.

"I 'ad ang urlly nii iii u-ay," he says through the toothpaste. Then he spits.

I steal a glance at him in the mirror. "Was that, 'I had a really nice time today'?"

He looks at me quizzically. "Maybe."

I drink a gallon of water to ward off certain death and then lie back in the bed. The mattress creaks as he joins me. He starts talking again about the agent woman he met, and I stare straight up at the ceiling. I could roll over and talk to him properly, but there is the smallest chance I might throw up.

It takes me a few moments to realize he's asked me a question.

"What do you mean, 'What about me?'" I say as it sinks in.

"What was Colin, the producer, saying to you?"

I force my brain to remember. "He was saying he would find me more interesting things to do."

"That's great!"

"Yeah, I was hoping maybe I might get to meet some of the writers and find out what they do. I've got this sort-of idea thing I'm working on." I stop, realizing what I've said. "It's probably crap."

I hear him shift over onto his side. "I'm sure it's not. I'd love to read it."

I turn onto my side away from him. "Night, night!"

"Gabi . . ."

I do a pretend snore.

His arm slips around me, and I realize my whole body is tense. "I'm going to pester you till you let me read it," he says. His breath on my neck makes me even more tense, but at the same time feel like I want to melt into him. We stay like that, and bit by bit I relax. This is what Max used to do when I got wound up. Just be there. And one by one, all my panicky thoughts would switch off.

It's strange being in the same situation with a different arm around me. He feels solid and there and like if I push him, he'll push back. Like he feels this could be something really special, and he won't give up at the first sign of trouble.

But how can you be sure?

I wake up an hour later and creep out to the bathroom, only treading a little bit on Spencer. I've got a pounding headache and I want to die.

When I come back in, he's awake. He asks me if I'm all right, and I tell him that it feels like tiny people are having a rock fight inside my skull.

"I know a good cure for a headache," he says, looking at me steadily with a hint of a grin.

I open my mouth, but can't think of anything to say and

119

shut it again, like a fish. I go over and sit on the bed and look at him. There's a wicked glint in his eye, and it makes me smile. I hardly know anything about him, but there's something drawing me in. I find it kind of exciting that he's a mystery.

I lean toward him and get a flutter of panic. Are we actually going to do anything? What if he's actually a dick and pulls this routine on every girl? Also, my boobs go all over the place when released. I didn't care with Max, but things with Spencer are different.

"I'm not ready to be number twenty-five just yet," I say quickly.

He grins. "I had something else in mind." He's moved off the bed and is standing in front of me. And at that moment I grab the front of his T-shirt and pull him toward me. We kiss, and his body is pressed between my legs, grazing up against me. He pushes me back on the bed, so I can feel the weight of him on me. As our kisses get harder, I pull at his hair, and I can hear our breathing get faster. He runs his hands over my legs, just missing the place where I feel I might explode. Then he pulls his head away from mine and, keeping eye contact, moves back down until he's kneeling by the side of the bed. He pushes the edge of my T-shirt up and kisses my stomach. He slides off my underwear, and his kisses keep on moving down. I freeze for a moment when I realize what's happening. This is definitely crossing over into something. Something . . . But soon it's difficult to think.

He's right—it does get rid of my headache.

Afterward he slides behind me and puts his arm around me.

"That was more than strictly friendly," I say.

"All part of the service," he says, sort of into my hair.

"You're just my tour guide, though," I say. "Don't go getting above yourself." He can't see how much I'm smiling.

"I wouldn't dream of it."

We spend the rest of the night curled up together. We just sort of fit. I don't sleep for a long time because millions of things are buzzing around in my brain, but mainly I want to stay in this moment for as long as possible.

CHAPTER 22

Spencer's gone when I wake up. And for a moment my heart plunges in my chest. Then I spot a note on the pillow. He's drawn a cup of tea on it.

It's a bit of a shock to look in the mirror and see how monumentally rough I look this morning. Then I remember the mugs of wine. At least I have an excuse for looking like a corpse. I don't have any makeup with me, so Spencer will just have to deal with it. It's best he sees my morning face now, really, just so he doesn't get a shock in the future. Assuming there is going to be some sort of future. I can't just pretend nothing happened last night, can I? Or that it wasn't a big deal.

This is going against my rules. I want to keep it fun. No thinking. If I want to run downstairs and kiss him now, that's what I'll do. I don't need to go all *Dawson's Creek* and analyze everything.

I pop my head around the banister and peer into the

kitchen on my way down the stairs. Spencer is on the phone, holding what looks like a business card. He's speaking too quietly for me to hear anything.

"Who was that?" I ask when he hangs up.

He laughs in a bit of a shocked way. "Don't be nosy."

That's pretty annoying. I thought we'd begin the day kissing and saying nice things to each other, not with secret phone calls. He passes me some tea, as if that will distract me. Actually, it does a bit.

Maybe if I kiss him, he will tell me. I put my cup down on the table and go over to him, slipping my arms around his neck.

He steps back and moves away from my mouth, sloshing his tea over his hand in the process.

I pull my arms away quickly. Flashes of panic are starting in the pit of my stomach. I hope I haven't just made an awful mistake.

"Gabi." He fixes me with a look I can't read. "Did you know you talk in your sleep?"

That throws me. The panic dies down slightly, but I still have no idea what's going on. "Yeah, M— A couple of people have mentioned it."

He frowns into his tea. What did I say? I know I've said "Max, I love your sexy body" a couple of times when I've been in bed with Mia. She only really minded when I put my leg over her at the same time. And once some stuff I said traumatized Mia's little brother, Matthew, when we were on that family camping trip. It can't be worse than that.

He's not grinning like I said something funny, though. He's frowning into his mug.

"You said, 'I love you, Max.'"

The words hit me like a block of ice in the chest.

He finishes off the tea in one swallow and turns away toward the sink.

"You should hear some of the stuff my friend Nish does in her sleep." My voice is coming out all singsong. "I'm nothing compared to her."

His mug clangs on the bottom of the sink and he walks back toward me. "Yeah? What does she do, then?" He smiles.

And with that he lets me off the hook.

CHAPTER 23

Spencer has to go to a meeting, so I walk back to the station on my own.

I can't help what I say in my sleep, can I? There's no point in feeling weird and guilty about it. And Spencer and I aren't even really together. It was just a bit of fun. Friends with benefits. All that stuff about liking him was just the alcohol playing tricks on my brain.

I don't really have the money to keep calling France, so I send Mia a text instead.

```
Sexy times with Spencer! Do you want
the deets? ;) x

No thanks, I'm eating x (But I am
happy for you.)
```

```
I sent you an FB message ;) x
```

```
Gross x
```

I kind of wish that I had gotten to actually speak to her. I'm making out like it wasn't a big deal, and like the sleep-talking thing was funny. I think I'll call home, though not to tell them about Spencer, obviously.

It's Saturday, so Dad will be making bacon bagels. He gets a little annoyed that Millie and I ask for bacon bagels all the time, because he can cook all kinds of amazing food. Julia should totally think about employing him at Radleigh, if he didn't have his job selling pipes or walls or whatever, that is. The pulled-pork thing he makes is way better than the one they have. But on the other hand, you can't beat a bit of bacon.

I'm not as bad as Max, though. The time he came over for dinner and told my parents that he liked eating ramen noodles with ketchup, I think Dad almost stabbed him with a fork.

"Hello?" says a voice.

Oh, no. I've got Millie on the landline.

"It's me. Can you put Mom on?"

"Ugh, you smell."

"Shut up, ugly. Put Mom on."

"I can, like, smell you from here."

"Shut up."

"It's like you've pooed yourself."

"What have you been doing? Missing me?"

"I changed Dad's Facebook status to say you were covered in hair."

"I know."

"Okayluvyabai."

"Wait! What about Dad? Can I speak to him?"

"Dad's crazy again. He's baking an assload of cakes."

"Don't say assload!"

"Okayluvyabai!"

She hangs up. Argh! She is so annoying. Next time we play the fighting game, I am really going to hurt her. I say "game," but it's just me and her fighting, really. With weapons. I think Mom and Dad were disappointed that we didn't just play with the dolls and stuff.

My phone rings. It's home. I hate my sister.

"Piss off, you asshat."

"Gabi?"

"Oh, hi, Dad!"

Talking to Dad was like being wrapped in a big warm blanket. He asked me all about the job and kept saying how impressive it was, even though I was mostly talking about getting coffee and photocopying things. When I told him I might have the chance to do something different, he said, "Ooooh," and asked what sort of thing. I said probably looking at trends and things. He said, "Ooooh," again, because I don't think he knew what I was talking about.

He was telling me about his job. He's back at work now after his break, and apparently Sue Someone placed the wrong order and Jacqui Something was going to tell her off but couldn't because of her hyperactive thigh. I think that's what he said. Dad's job is very boring, but he likes to talk about it a lot and we all pretend to listen, except Millie, who tells him to stop boring her. Because she is fourteen. And a demon.

When I told him about the girls visiting and us going to a house party, he paused for a moment before saying, "No boys."

"Dad!"

"You should focus on the summer. And your friends. Don't bother with men—they'll only annoy you."

"Should I tell Mom not to bother with you, then?"

"Oh, I annoy your mom all the time. I mean it, though. You should have a break after Max. Focus on you."

I told him that boys were the last thing on my mind, and ignored the tiny bubble of guilt at the lie as I thought of last night.

I also asked if he wanted to come visit me in London, but he said it wasn't a good time at the moment, so I made him promise to send me a bacon bagel. He didn't technically agree to, but I told him if he really loved me, he would find a way.

When I hang up, I look around and have no idea where I am. I'd wandered off from Spencer's and have ended up on a bridge over a canal. It's pretty, though, with a golden glint on the water from the morning sun.

I stand there staring down at the water for a while and think how difficult it is to sort one thought from another.

I want to see him, but at the same time I want to run away.

CHAPTER 24

Shooting starts at midday, so it doesn't really seem worth going back to Granny's. I text her to say I will see her tonight. Her reply doesn't make any sense and is mostly nonsense words, because I think she's texting while out for a run. I wonder what people with no friends do in London.

When I arrive on location, Spencer is already there. He's talking to Heidi and the director, Mark. I'm sure his eyes dart in my direction as I go past, so I wave, but he seems not to have seen me. Why is he even here? He shot his line the other day. I know he's in the background for lots of scenes, but still.

At my desk (a little shelf where I put my things) there's a note waiting for me.

Gabie.

Please stop putting coffee in plastic cups. They injure my
hands. I would like paper cups from now on.
Regards,
Heidi

Well, that's rude. And wrong. How hard is it to spell
Gabi? And who writes "Regards" on a Post-it? I don't have
any paper cups. God, I want to kill people.

Then I see Angry Skull wandering around outside,
talking to Heidi and a woman I've seen a few times, who I
think is one of the writers. Spencer is still over there, and it
looks like he's being handed a script. He must have given
Heidi my name, though not the additional brain cells to
spell it. I want to talk to Angry Skull about the more interesting things I might get to do. Would he think it was bad
if I didn't provide paper cups for his star actress, though?
It could come across as if I was deliberately injuring her
hands. There must be something I can do.

The square outside the main university buildings holds
what seems to be some sort of Saturday market. As I head
over, it looks promising, though I must not get distracted
by the smell of meat. I walk through, absorbing the hum
of chatter interrupted by sounds of sizzling from the stalls.
There are olive stalls, stands piled high with cheese, a man
selling bacon bagels—a whiff from that one nearly wipes all
thoughts of the cup mission from my mind.

The aroma of coffee beans keeps poking through all
of the other smells, and eventually I track down the stall
it's coming from. The man standing behind it looks only
slightly older than me. His name tag says "Felix," so I'm

guessing he's Spanish. He also looks Spanish and the stall is called A Taste of Spain. Could I tell him it's a strange English custom to give free paper cups to women?

"Excuse me," I say, loudly and slowly.

"Yes, madam?" he says. In a London accent. I won't be able to fool him with made-up English traditions. I'll have to just ask.

"Could I borrow one of your cups?"

"Will you bring it back?"

"No."

He laughs. "Then you can *have* one of my cups. Can I ask why?"

"I'm working on the TV show filming over there. I have to give people coffee, and someone says that plastic cups injure her hands."

I show him the note.

"So you're . . . Gabie?"

"I'm Gabi, without the 'e.' I didn't think it was that tricky to spell. Although once when I got a coffee at Starbucks they'd written what looked like 'Nip' on it."

He laughs again and hands me a stack of paper cups and plastic lids for them. I shove them into my handbag, checking the time on my phone. Shooting won't have started yet. It's good I arrived early, even if the reason for it was that I have no friends and nothing to do.

"Thanks so much," I say.

"Wait a sec," Felix replies, and I see he's started making a coffee. He steams the milk, puts on the lid, and holds it out to me. "This one's for you. Tell your friends to come to A Taste of Spain."

"I don't have any friends."

"Oh." The pause is awkward.

"But when I do make some, I'll tell them!"

"Great!" He looks relieved—probably because I'm leaving.

I hurry back out of the square, across the road, and onto campus. The same group is still standing there talking. Heidi sees me.

"Oh, you got my note. Great!" She gives me a huge grin. Then she reaches for the nice coffee with the steamed milk. I hold on to it just a second too long, but she gives a firm tug and then she has it. I catch Spencer's eye. For a moment my heart leaps, getting a brief image of last night, but the feeling falters a bit when I think of the morning.

"Thanks," Heidi chimes in and winks at me.

"Gabi." It's Angry Skull talking. "Do you have five minutes? I thought I'd set up some meetings for you."

Spencer shifts from one foot to the other and looks down. I'm sure I see a frown cross his face.

"Yes, sure." I try to stop thinking about what Spencer is doing and focus. "I just have to make the drinks, so after that?"

"I can talk to you while you do that. Lead the way."

As he follows me into the university building, I hear Heidi's voice ring out behind me.

"Why does my cup have 'Nip' written on it?"

It was another one of Max's and my stupid arguments about nothing. We always had them. Like the time I told him he put his socks on in a really annoying way, and he shouted, "I literally don't know what you mean!" Or when he was in a bad mood because he fell over while putting on his pants and I couldn't stop laughing, even though he hit his head on the floor and it "could have been really serious." But this argument didn't feel like it was about nothing.

I'd invited him over for a night in together. My parents were out, and we were going to cook dinner. Rosie had been on a date with this guy who'd taken her out to dinner, and they'd gotten all dressed up and it was really romantic. So I told Max we needed to do something nice, because we never bothered to do anything except watch TV and play Call of Duty. *Max kept saying that I should take it easy after all the family stuff that happened and stop trying to organize things, but I told him not to be stupid. I was fine.*

I know it was hard, because I was working almost every Saturday night, and some Fridays, at Radleigh, and he was under lots of pressure from his dad to study for his exams because he was probably going to get good grades, unlike me. Max's dad said events management was a Mickey Mouse subject.

And everyone was asking us (mostly in a mocking way) when the big day was going to be, and I started feeling like no one saw us as a real couple. I told Max he had to be there early so we could go shopping for ingredients. He showed up late and brought his PlayStation with him.

I was trying to make a list of food by flipping through a cookbook.

"Ooh, babe, we could make chicken in prosciutto!"

"Die, fleshbag!"

"This Thai red curry looks good."

Max was suspiciously quiet. Then I heard crunching.

"Are you eating?"

Crunch. "Hmm?"

"What are you eating?"

There was a silence, and then he said something that sounded like, "A snub of shitbits."

"What the hell is a snub of shitbits?"

"A TUB of TWIGLETS!"

I went off, shouting at him for not making an effort and not bothering to wear nice clothes when I knew he'd gotten a new T-shirt for a night out with his friends. And for eating snacks when I was cooking a nice meal. He didn't respond. Then I went over to the front of the sofa and saw that he'd put on headphones. So I ripped the PlayStation plug out of the wall. He dropped the controller in horror.

"Oh my God, don't be a bitch about it or anything!"

"You weren't listening." I flung my arm out at him in anger.

"If you were reading a book, I wouldn't come along and . . . burn it!"

"That doesn't make sense!"

"Yeah, I guess it doesn't. Because when would you ever be reading a book?"

It felt like a slap. I kicked the Twiglets over.

"Oh, 'cause you're such an intellectual, Max. All you've read are all the Harry Potter books and that thing with all the hairy children and the frog man."

"*The Lord of the Rings?*"

"*Whatever. I planned a nice night for us, and you come over looking all scruffy. And then you're rude.*"

"*Why are you being all weird? Normally you'd be playing too, wearing your pajamas and not talking to me as though you're my mom.*"

He did have a point. I usually changed into my pajamas as soon as I got in the house. Especially if I knew it was just Max coming over.

He reattached the PlayStation, set the Twiglet tub upright again, and dug out another handful.

"*STOP EATING TWIGLETS!*"

He got another handful and slowly and deliberately crammed them into his mouth.

"*Who eats a whole tub of Twiglets anyway? Why can't you just put a reasonable amount in a little bag before you come over? WHAT'S WRONG WITH YOU? Are you some kind of monster?*"

Max cracked up. "*Why can't I just put a reasonable amount in a little bag? Can you hear yourself?*"

The point where the argument descended into laughter was usually where it ended. And that's what Max thought was happening, because he hugged me. Saying "*Get off*" *and wriggling just made him hug me tighter, stroke my hair, and say,* "*Ah, love. We're in love,*" *in a silly voice.*

"*I'm really sorry I was a dick,*" *he said then.*

There was the familiar Max-y smell. My face was squashed against his chest.

Then he whispered, "*Gabi . . .*" *and I turned my face toward his.*

And he burped.

I shoved him away. "You're so disgusting."

"Ah, it's just you. Like you've ever cared before."

As he squeezed me tighter, a cold, numb feeling—one that always seemed to be in the pit of my stomach those days—grew. My whole body felt hollow. I knew I was about to say something awful.

CHAPTER 25

The whole set is in a state of confusion and chaos the next day because we've just been told that a brand new scene needs to be shot at the end of the day. When I was photocopying the scripts to hand out, I saw that Spencer was in it.

Apparently it was decided that Harry and Jas didn't have enough tension between them. There needed to be something more to keep them apart.

Now Jas is going to go all wild and hook up with a random guy at a bar—Spencer. His character has gone from Student in Bar 1 to Hugh, who is a rich, bad boy. I can't wait to make fun of him about it—that is, if I see him. I haven't been able to speak to him at all today.

And I've kind of been avoiding him.

Lots of work needs to be done dressing the set in one of the student bars downstairs, which is used as the club. I've been spending hours on the phone trying to get hold of the actor who plays the bartender to let him know he needs to come back in.

People keep going up to Spencer and congratulating him. Most of the time Heidi is with him. They're still talking through the scene right up until the last minute, barely noticing the various people coming over to touch up their makeup and arrange strands of hair around Spencer's face—strands of his own hair, I mean; they weren't adding extra ones.

When the cameras roll, I'm not actually there. I have to be upstairs to stop random people from coming in. But I have the script with me. I made one too many copies.

The scene starts with Jas downing shots. I wonder if Heidi will ask for the shots to be served in paper shot glasses. It would be a shame if she injured her hands. Rich, bad Hugh is leaning against a wall at the back of the club. He's wearing a white T-shirt with one of those checked scarves wound around his neck, and they were talking about keeping him in his hat. The cast have all been complaining about the warm winter clothes they have to wear.

So Jas's friends point out Hugh, who "glowers moodily." Jas shouts that she's done with men for good and that he looks like a grumpy bastard, at which point Spencer has to do his first piece of acting and raise an eyebrow. Jas gets more drunk, and then Hugh comes over and offers her drugs. When she says no, he says, "Or perhaps you'd like something even more . . . intoxicating." But Jas walks off, straight into Harry, who is kissing a girl. So Jas marches back over to Hugh, grabs him, and kisses him, right in the middle of the club.

I imagine he'll softly brush her lips at first. And then move against her more forcefully. And the tip of his tongue will meet hers. And he'll kiss her deeply and passionately and it will all be stupid and perfect.

I seem to have crumpled the script into a ball.

I try to pick out sounds in the murmur coming from downstairs, but I can't figure out which part of the scene they're doing. But when the noise dips, I'm sure that must be the kiss.

The noise dips five times.

CHAPTER 26

I think filming in the bar has got everyone in a party mood. They come walking up the stairs, and Bex, who plays mean Jen but is totally lovely in real life, calls out to me to say that they're heading to the pub and tells me where it is so I can come along after I help clean up.

I'm worried that I won't get in. At Spanky's, the bouncers are total pervs and just let us in anyway. They must know we're underage. But when I reach the pub I see there aren't any bouncers at this place.

Maybe I should ask somebody else to get my drink, though. Mainly because there are about five billion people at the bar and I don't care to wait. Someone nudges my arm.

"Heyy, Gaaab." Spencer is grinning at me. He's definitely a bit drunk.

"Hello."

"You've been ignoring me today." He points his finger at me.

"I haven—"

"I feel used."

He's making his quizzical frown face with one eyebrow raised. Then he pouts. In a husky voice he says, "Would it help if I was bad-boy Hugh?" His voice drops even lower, so that it's barely audible to human ears. "D'you want some *drugs*, Gabi?" He does the eyebrow thing again, waggling it up and down this time.

I can't stop the laugh from coming out, and the little voice in my head telling me to run gets quieter.

Then he says, "Have this drink," and hands me his beer. "We've got a whole table of them over there." He beckons me away from the bar area and into a corner.

"So how did it all happen, then?" I ask as we head over. His personality transformation has me on edge. I don't know how to be around him.

"I, um, signed up with that agent." He speaks quickly. "She has tons of contacts at the company. She e-mailed Colin and Mark after she saw me on Friday. Said the show was missing a real bad boy. Apparently the new big thing is 'tall, dark . . . *stubbly*, and bad,' which is me—or so she says."

"You are stubbly," I agree.

He grins and grabs another beer from the table.

I wonder if I should say anything about last night. Or this morning.

Or I could kiss him and forget about anything big and just enjoy myself.

I'm leaning forward when a hand appears on his shoulder. It's Heidi. I don't think she even notices I'm there. She's dragging Spencer onto the dance floor, saying, "Cast song!"

They're all standing in a circle with their arms around each other and are opening up to let Spencer in. But he stops.

"Wait a minute." He takes a step back toward me and holds out his hand to pull me into the circle with him. Bex cheers, and some of the other cast do too, even though they probably don't know my name. The girl who plays Priya puts her arm around me, but all I can think about is Spencer's hand on my waist. The song is "We Are Young" by Fun, and we all sway in the circle, really going for it when it gets to the chorus. At the "na na" part, Spencer and I sing it into each other's faces, trying to outdo each other. When the final "tonight" rings out, we throw our arms upward and whoop.

Spencer puts his arm around me again, lifts me up, and spins me in a circle. I'm dizzy and laughing and feel a bit more like the old me from last year, before all the sad stuff happened. I think some people are looking over—I do have a pretty loud laugh—but I don't really care.

When he stops, I slide back down his body until my feet touch the floor, but he holds me close and leans his head forward.

"Do you want to come back?"

"Better not stay out two nights this weekend. Granny will go nuts," I say. There's a happy hum going through me that he wants me to come over again.

"It'll be a shame if you go," he mutters, swaying slightly.

I take a step back. "I know what's going on here," I say. "You lurve me."

He laughs. "Oh *do* I?"

"Yeah, obviously. It's okay—I don't blame you."

He fiddles with a strand of hair on my shoulder. "Do you really have to go home?"

"People might start thinking we're more than tourist and tour guide."

Something—maybe disappointment—flashes across his face before he regains his composure and shakes his head. "We wouldn't want that."

In the background I notice a girl standing by the bar. She has long, ringletty red hair, and I recognize her as one of the extras. Her eyes are fixed on Spencer, and suddenly a thought snags in my brain, a feeling tugging at me and telling me that if I miss an opportunity to see him, he will lose interest. And there are those flashes of panic again. This must be what happens when people go out with someone new and then they disappear and you hardly see them. A few minutes ago I wasn't thinking about anything except having fun with Spencer, and now I feel like I need to be with him.

It scares me.

"You can take your pick of the girls now that you're an acting hunk," I say, and take a gulp of beer.

"Um, I guess." Spencer frowns at me. He takes a step back as well.

"What about that girl over there?" I point out the

red-haired girl by the bar. "She's been looking you over."

"You want me to go hit on that girl?" He fixes me with an intense look.

I shrug. "Yeah, why not?"

What am I *doing*?

He doesn't say anything and takes another sip of his drink, still watching me.

"So I'm going to go," I say.

Spencer nods. "Cool. Well, I'll walk you out."

He turns abruptly to go, and I follow him a few paces behind. We walk stiffly, as though the chilly mood between us is affecting our movement.

I don't know what's making me do this—push him as far away as possible. It's as if I'm trying to prove to myself that I can't trust him.

As we come out the door we hear raised voices. One is high-pitched and, although it's more strained than usual, is unmistakably Heidi Adams. She's standing by a taxi on the street outside the pub and arguing with a man in a suit who has very square hair.

She's shrieking, "It's *not* fair! We only had a few drinks!"

His voice is low and quiet and a little scary. "Heidi, you have work in the morning. You have auditions this week. What's 'not fair' is you taking advantage of my money."

We've stopped right by them. Heidi sees us and flinches, a mortified expression passing over her face. Then she flashes us a smile. "Guys! Going home together? That's adorable."

"Everything all right, Heidi?" Spencer frowns.

"Um, yeah. I hope you have an early night, Spence. I want you in shape for our scene." She pokes him playfully on the shoulder and grins again. Although I feel sorry for her, I would still like to hit her.

"Get in the car," says the man to Heidi, ushering her in. He hasn't even turned to look at us.

After the brief chance to think about something else, we turn back to each other.

"So you'll be all right getting to the station?" There's a thaw in his voice. It makes me want to take back all the stupid stuff I was saying about other girls.

But I don't. I nod, and all the confused feelings about him jumble around inside me.

"Well, I'll . . ." He points behind him back into the pub. There's a pause. This is my chance to keep him here.

It passes. The only noise is a far-off siren.

I stay rooted to the spot as I watch him go. From here I can see back into the pub. I can see him go in. See him talking to the red-haired girl. See him slip his arm around her waist as they disappear off together into the crowd.

It's for the best, I tell myself. It takes the pressure off. And now I know that if I push him away, he'll go.

But I wish it were me he had his arm around.

I hadn't noticed that I'm shivering. I have no idea what the time is. I take out my phone to check for messages before I lose signal on the train. I have a whole bunch of messages and missed calls. Granny must be paranoid, but I'm not going to be back very late.

It's only when I look closer that I see the calls aren't from Granny; they're from Nish.

Oh my God. Today was Rosie's birthday.

CHAPTER 27

I keep trying to focus on feeling bad and writing my I'M REALLY SORRY e-mail, because I do feel awful. Granny keeps calling for me to come down from my ladder room for breakfast. She's going to come up in a minute and see what's wrong; it's highly unusual for me to not appear when food is on the table.

But I keep clicking over onto the Facebook photos of Rosie's birthday night out. I've scrolled through the same thirty-eight pictures probably a million times. There is a ball of guilt and jealousy sitting in the pit of my stomach. The worst thing is, I think I'm more upset that Max is in the pictures than I am guilty about what I did.

Max was at Rosie's birthday. I know it doesn't make sense to be so annoyed. I'm angry with him for doing exactly the same thing I am. Going out and having a good time. Focusing on himself and friends, like Dad said I should do.

But the way it all looks—how happy and smiley and laughy he is, dancing with everyone, with his arm around Rosie—all makes it seem as if he doesn't get randomly sad about us, like I do. He's right there, making his stupid comedic pout that he does in photos, his arm around Rosie, their cheeks touching.

It's stupid, but I feel like I've got a right to know about everything that happens in his life. And when I go back through Max's photos, I realize that last Saturday Rosie went out for Max's brother, Cal's, birthday. There she is, with Max again, not tagged in any of the pictures.

Surely if she wasn't doing anything wrong, she wouldn't have untagged herself—and she would also have mentioned that she was going there when she left last week.

Also, I've tried to call her five times to apologize for missing the party, but she hasn't picked up. I don't know what to do. At the same time, I think that if she does answer, I might ask her about Max . . . and I don't think I can take it if she just says that I've got no right to get upset at what Max does anymore.

I've got too many thoughts in my head, and I want to scream. I can't concentrate on feeling angry because I feel guilty, and vice versa. People keep flashing in front of my eyes. Spencer. Max. Rosie. Dad. I'm pacing around and must be causing enough of a commotion for Granny to hear, because her head appears through the trapdoor. For a woman of sixty-five, she's pretty nimble on the ladder.

"What's going on up here, eh?" she says softly.

I sit down on the bed, close Facebook, and plaster a big grin on my face. "Nothing! I'm fine." Then I turn back to the screen, because she's coming toward me with her suspicious look.

She sits next to me on the bed, puts her arm around me, and gives me a squeeze.

"It's nothing to be ashamed of if you have a wobbly moment. You've been through a lot this year."

"Don't worry, Granny," I say. But I tilt my head toward her and lean on her shoulder. We sit there for a while, not saying anything.

When she's climbing back down the ladder she pauses. "You'll take things slowly with this boy, won't you? Make sure he's not a bastard."

CHAPTER 28

Spencer arrives on location in shades and is looking a little paler than usual.

He immediately comes over to talk to me and I get a rush of warmth for him, even though I know he probably went off with that girl.

"I feel like I've been hit in the face with a brick," he groans. I smile at him and feel a bit lighter. It's nice talking to someone who doesn't know anything about the stuff with my friends. But I still find it really hard to concentrate. When something is unresolved, it gnaws away at me. It stops me from eating or doing anything normal. I'm actually relieved that my meeting with the editor and the writer gets postponed by Colin. He'd forgotten that today is the day I have to dress up as a giant condom.

Before long I'm walking through the corridors of the university building carrying a cardboard box full of sexual health leaflets and (normal-sized) condoms to the set for me and my fellow giant-condom people to hand out. But with no food and gallons of coffee, I'm feeling shaky. My arms feel like they're hollow. Then the box slips through my hands, and the *thump* of it hitting the floor echoes off the walls. It lands on its side and all the leaflets spill out, scooting along the floor with a *whoosh*. I feel like kicking the box, but I breathe in and sink down to my knees to pick everything up.

I crumple some of the leaflets in my frustration and then stop and sit back on my heels. I need to get a grip. These are for a scene. This is my job. No one on the show is going to care if I'm feeling crappy because I forgot my friend's birthday and am jealous about her hanging out with my ex.

That thought is a little sad. I don't have a person here to bitch and whine to without worrying that they'll think I'm mean. Max was like my anchor, keeping me secure in the knowledge that I couldn't be too awful a person because, like Mia, he saw all my worst parts and still liked me. Now I feel as though I'm wading around, never sure how to be.

As I pick up the last flyer, I hear the rumble of voices farther down the corridor. The deep one I'm sure is Spencer's. For a moment I think I can feel the vibrations through the floor, but it's probably footsteps—although Spencer's "bad-boy Hugh" voice is very deep. The high, shrill one is most likely Heidi's. I get up and haul the box with me as they round the corner.

Spencer is wearing a pastel-pink shirt. He has something over his arm, which I think might be a vest. It's a shame that landing his dream role also involves looking like a total douche. He walks up to me and holds out a piece of paper. It's one of my sex leaflets, along with a condom.

"Yours?" He grins.

"Yep." I take them from him and then struggle to hold the box with one hand so I can drop them in. He puts his hand out to take the weight of the box.

"Are you okay?" His eyebrows are crooked, but it looks like genuine concern.

"I'm fine. Are you still hungover?"

His face is pained. "Very," he whispers.

"Come on, Spence," chirps Heidi. "We're going to be called soon." She practically grabs him and drags him away from me.

He hands me back the full weight of the box and nods at me.

"Good luck with your scene!" I call after him.

I'm on set and in costume before I know it. All I have to do is hand out leaflets and chant "NLU Sex Week," over and over again, but avoid saying it in time with the other condoms. I am not the condom who will actually hand the leaflet to Tom, who's reeling from the news that he's gotten a girl pregnant from a one-night stand last season. That's Condom 1, played by a girl named Lorna. I think her parents have turned up to watch. I don't think many people realize that Condom 2 is the girl who brings them coffee.

I'm absolutely boiling. Summer is in full force, and I almost wish the costume was made of actual condom material rather than thick nylon, except then it would be see-through, and I'm only wearing a bra and jeans underneath.

They didn't tell me that the costume had no arms, so I had to take off my short-sleeved shirt. It's also really heavy, and it takes a lot of effort not to sag.

When Mark yells "Action!" everyone starts milling around, and I spot Spencer out of the corner of my eye. He's very subtly recording the scene on his phone. When Mark calls for another take, I shoot Spencer A Look, and he puts the phone back into his pocket and puts up his hands in surrender. Then the moment passes, and one of the writers starts talking to him and showing him a script.

The sun is beating down on my bare arms, and I didn't put any sunscreen on. When this goes out on TV I'll be red. And squinting. It's exciting to actually be part of the show, but all I really want is to go inside and see if anyone has replied to my I'M REALLY SORRY e-mail and texts.

After half an hour I never want to say "NLU Sex Week" ever again. Which is good, really, because I probably won't have to. We're all gathered together to have some promotional pictures taken. They're going to release a teaser campaign revealing that there's a pregnancy, but not saying who it is. So we take pictures with different cast members while they all make an "OMG surprise baby" face. When it's Heidi's turn she strikes her pose, but a gust of wind blows a bit of crap into my eye, which makes me screw my face up at just the wrong moment. Let's hope no one looks at Condom 2 in that picture.

And then my fun is over and I'm back to being a normal runner. I check my phone. No reply to my messages yet. Tomorrow Rosie will get the I'M SORRY chocolate gift I ordered. It's this chocolate plaque on which you can get a personal message written in icing, so I asked for "I'm sorry" in capital letters.

I'm late for collecting the lunch orders, so I need to get out of the condom costume as soon as possible. I hurry back to the prop room, although "hurry" is a bit of an exaggeration—the leg holes at the bottom of the costume are very small, so it's more of a hobble. I start unzipping the costume in the corridor, thinking that black skinny jeans were a huge mistake today. I am actually dying of heat.

Spencer is sitting at a desk in the prop room reading his script, and he jumps out of his skin when I come limping in. He's still looking at me wide-eyed as I explain, all out of breath, "Sorry! Need to get the lunch orders."

Then I realize that the reason he's staring is that I'm emerging from my costume with no top on. I was so hot that I'd totally forgotten. The costume is hanging around my waist now, and I'm standing there in my bra.

Spencer's face breaks into a grin. But before he can say anything, we hear voices coming from outside the room—voices that I immediately recognize as belonging to the director, Mark, and Angry Skull. And they're getting louder and closer.

I start trying to pull the costume up over my hips again, but it's all twisted around the wrong way and gets stuck, so I yank it down and step out of it. That doesn't help the topless problem, though. Seeing as I heard that a runner got fired for getting the tea order wrong, I don't want to be caught half-naked in the prop room with a boy.

Spencer springs up and runs to the side of the room

where there's a walk-in closet. The voices are just outside the door. I sprint over just as Spencer opens the closet door and launch myself at the opening. He steps in after me and pulls the door closed.

Footsteps and voices enter the room. Shadows disrupt the crack of light at the bottom of the closet door as they talk.

Other than that, it's pitch black in here. I can barely see Spencer's outline. But I can hear his quick breathing underneath the deafening pounding of my heart.

I turn at the same moment he does and we're kissing. Our lips move forcefully, as though we're fighting to get as close as possible to each other. His T-shirt brushes against the bare skin of my stomach, sending shivers all over me. His hands are on my waist and my back and then my hair. All over I'm burning for him, and I don't want it to stop.

I tried to arrange things to do together the week after Max and I broke up. I wanted to prove that all the people who said we'd find it really difficult to be friends so soon were wrong. We went for a meal. At first it felt like nothing had changed, but every so often something would happen that would make it awkward. Like when his mom called and didn't tell him to say hi to me. Or when the old man at the next table called us lovebirds. When stuff like that happened, it was as if the air around us turned sad. Max got tears in his eyes at one point, and I saw him trying to get rid of them without me seeing. That made it so much worse. Every time I think of him crying I'm absolutely racked with guilt, because I remember him crying when I broke up with him, when he realized what I was saying and all he said was, "No."

The following week I got him to come over and watch a movie. Because I was nervous I ended up being really formal about it and told him that dinner was at seven and the film would commence at eight. He put his hand on my arm and said, "Chill out." We both knew we'd actually be eating chips and ice cream at random points throughout the night while watching a reality dating show, because that's what we would normally do.

It seemed to work. Everything felt normal and not sad. We even got over it pretty quickly when Millie came into my room, looked at us, said, "Well, this is weird," and walked out.

When Max looked at the clock it was way past midnight. Dad had already knocked on the door to ask how Max was getting home, and we called back that he was going to walk.

"Just stay!" I blurted out when it came to it.

"What, here?" Max frowned.

"Yeah! I mean, we've shared a bed a million times. It won't be weird. It'll be normal."

His expression was unsure. "Um, okay. So, should we turn around while we get changed?"

I hadn't even thought about that; I'd just started taking off my jeans. He saw that and turned to face the wall. So I turned to face the other wall.

"Sorry, I don't really know the new rules," he muttered.

"Ready!" I said, putting in a lot of effort to keep up the feeling that this was all fine and normal.

"That's my shirt."

"What? Oh, well, yeah. But I always wear it." I'd forgotten that the Barcelona jersey I wear in bed isn't technically mine.

"I want it back."

"Max, don't be a jerk." I half laughed, and then I saw his face. He looked really annoyed. Usually in arguments I was the annoyed one. I'd rant and rave about how much he stressed me out, and he'd just laugh at me.

I got a strange, horrible pang in the pit of my stomach.

"I was going to take it with me when I go to London," I said. "Something to remind me of you." My voice went all weird and shaky.

"Why do you want to be reminded of me now?" he said in a low voice. "I'm just another one of your friends."

"One of my best friends. My closest friend. That actually means a lot." There was anger creeping into my voice now. How dare he make out like I didn't care about him? He couldn't cast me as the bad person and him as the victim. It wasn't fair.

"Are you going to give me back my fucking shirt?" he said nastily.

"Fine. Turn around," I snapped.

He did as he was told. I took the shirt off, put another one on, and then rolled the Barcelona one into a ball and threw it as hard as I could at his back. He spun around, his face twisted in anger. He picked up the shirt and flung it down on the floor. He picked it up again and threw it down again. And kept doing it. His whole body was tensed with rage. I could tell he wanted to pick up something more satisfying to throw, but everything around him was mine. I ran over and tried to get it from his hand.

"Stop being crazy!"

When my hand touched his arm I couldn't tell which of us was hotter. We were both burning. He stopped, but his arms stayed tense and his fists clenched. As we looked at each other, a familiar pull seemed to move us closer.

He put his other hand tentatively on my shoulder and all the fury in me changed to a deep, aching longing. It was like a hook, dragging me on. In perfect synchronization, we moved together and kissed. Even as I kissed him, a million confused thoughts flitted through my brain. I wanted him, but at the same time I didn't. I just wanted to cling to him, and for everything to feel normal. I grabbed onto his hair and then started randomly thinking about how he must have gotten a haircut and not told me.

My head was all over the place, but my body was taking over. I fell back onto the bed and pulled him with me. He pushed against me, and for a second I could feel him hard right on the place where I wanted him, and a ripple of pleasure ran through me. He pulled back slightly and started to kiss my neck, and his hand slid up my thigh.

The next thought I had was that the shorts I was wearing were also his. It was as though the same thought struck him at the same time. His hand froze, and he pulled his head up.

The spell was broken.

Max got up and stepped backward, rubbing the back of his head, his expression split between anger and confusion. "I don't think that's part of the new rules."

"No," I whispered.

"I'm going to go."

My dad had waited up in the kitchen, and when he heard me walking Max downstairs he offered to drive him home. This time, Max went.

CHAPTER 29

We emerge from the closet as if we're in a scene in a movie, looking around guiltily and smoothing down our clothes. Spencer gives me the vest to wear as a top.

We stand still and look at each other for a moment. And then start to laugh.

Gradually the laughter subsides, but the atmosphere between us still pulses.

"You know, I didn't get with that girl," he says suddenly.

Delight, relief, and a strange, unknown feeling surge through me.

"I was going to," he admits, "but someone else was on my mind."

It's as if tiny cracks are appearing in the wall I've put up against him. And I'm not rushing to fill them.

Spencer's script is poking out the top of his bag. The whole time we've been eating our sandwiches and talking about something—possibly a band or a book—I've been looking at it.

I finally agreed to a date with him: picnic on our lunch break. Another tiny step into uncertain territory, but it feels okay to take it. So far I haven't freaked out.

"Can I read it?" I ask.

"Okay." He leans across the blanket and pulls his bag over by the strap. "But you can't tell any—"

"OH MY GOD! YOU'RE HAVING SEX WITH JAS!"

"Shut up!" He laughs and tries to reach over and grab the script from me.

"But, oh my God! That means Harry and—"

He leans over again and this time manages to pry the pages from my hands. I think he might actually be annoyed.

"It's not like there's anyone around!" I protest. "Unless that squirrel happens to be a fan of *The Halls*."

He's still trying to look stern, but I see a smile twitch at the corner of his mouth.

"Am I annoying you?"

He's forcing the smile down again, trying to keep his frown, but his eyes are sparkling.

"Yes, you're very annoying. But the most annoying thing is"—he looks down and then up at me again with his eyebrows crooked—"that it makes me want to kiss you."

I think I might melt.

He leans forward tentatively, gauging my reaction. I'm

doing my best not to go crazy-eyed and say, "Yes, please." I think I'll look demure instead. What do demure people do? I think they look sort of sad.

He stops leaning in and looks a little worried—probably because he was about to kiss me and I suddenly looked really depressed. I give a big grin to show him I'm okay. He looks really confused now. I am ruining this. This is potentially the beginning of falling in love. It's like a scene from the show.

Oh, it's okay, he's leaning in again.

Wait a minute. *But the most annoying thing is that it makes me want to kiss you?*

"That's a line from the show!"

He stops and bites his lip. "Do you know every god-damn line from the show?"

"YES."

He leans back and laughs to himself. "You make this very difficult. How about I just kiss you to shut you up?"

"Well, I don't know about that." I barely pause. "Okay, go on, then."

He grabs the back of my head and kisses me softly. Moving forward slowly, he pushes his body between my knees as I relax. This time I can't think about anything else except wanting to feel his weight on me. I pull at his T-shirt, and he gently pushes me back onto the grass.

Spencer stops kissing me for a moment and looks down at me. His curly hair falls over his face.

"Let's go out."

"Do you mean like boyfriend and girlfriend?"

"Yep."

I breathe in sharply. Just see it as another tiny step. I look at him.

"Okay."

The sunlight comes creeping through the window in the morning, and I turn my head and look back at Spencer. His lips are slightly parted, and his curly hair is all messy on the pillow.

We came back to his house last night and talked. For the first time since we met, the conversation was direct—going straight for those big, scary subjects and trying not to flinch too much.

I told him what happened six months ago, when it all fell apart. When my family went to pieces and I was the one who had to hold it all together. How I told everyone I was fine, and how I'm too scared to let someone really know me. And that it's easier to push people away.

The only thing I didn't tell him was about the person who was there through it all. The one I did push away.

Spencer put his arms around my waist then. "You kept pushing me, but I'm still here."

I watch his eyelids begin to flutter open. I move my head, staying in the spooning position, and kiss him on the lips. I feel him tense in surprise, and then his hand moves up to my face as he pushes his lips onto mine. My body is still facing away from his, and he brushes his fingers lightly over the front of me, all the way down and then back up again. And down, and then back up. The lightness of his touch makes me squirm, and I feel like I might explode. I take his hand and move it down, and I feel him shift and grow hard against me. He moves his hand away, and I feel him turn behind me. There's the sound of him fumbling with a drawer as he finds a condom. It's only a few seconds, but the wait feels agonizing. And then it's happening. It's him—the smell of his skin, the feel of his lips—and it feels new, different.

I put my hand up on the headboard to push back against him as he slides in and out, still touching me softly at the same time. The sweet feeling builds and spreads until I want to cry out. I turn to kiss him again, and just as our lips meet, I start to shudder against him.

It's different and new in a way I couldn't have imagined.

CHAPTER 30

The next day, I hand around the coffees, catching Spencer's eye as I give him his. The air crackles between us.

Later, as I walk back with the lunch orders, I think I'm getting a bit of a tan after my day in the park yesterday. I feel light as I walk. I'm almost skipping. I got an I Forgive You text from Rosie and I'm meeting Spencer in the closet at lunchtime.

The hour before lunch creeps by painfully slowly. At one point I bash my phone with my hand because I think the time might be frozen, but no. When everyone has their food, there are still ten minutes to go until one o'clock, so I just go and get into the closet early. I probably should be doing something useful instead of just standing in the dark and waiting, but I don't. And Spencer finds it only a little scary when he joins me. He'll have to get used to me being eager.

He's all psyched for his scene later—his *lurve* scene, as

I call it. I've brought it up a lot since I found out about it. I think I'm a bit obsessed with it.

In the middle of kissing me, I say—sort of into his mouth—"Do you know your lines?"

He pulls back, but his hands are still in my hair. "There aren't many lines . . ."

"Okay, do you know your *actions*?"

He sighs and moves his hands down. Now I want to grab them back and pull him to me and squeeze him. I wish I knew how to not be insane.

"Okay, so she comes in. And then I say, 'Of all the gin joints . . .'" He says it in the deepest voice ever—like a cartoon villain—but the vibrations of his voice still cause tingles.

"And she says, 'Shut up,' and walks up to him and kisses him." He stops, as if waiting for me to kiss him. But I'm thinking.

"You should move her hair out of her face."

"Really?"

"Yeah, and don't tell them you're going to do it."

"Before or after the clothes come off?"

"After."

"Okay."

He steps forward and cups my face in his hands, kissing me hard. The force of it sends me backward and then we're up against the closet wall. Then he stops and brushes my hair out of my eyes with his fingers.

"And, cut," he says with a grin, knowing it will drive me crazy.

* * *

When lunch break is over, I step out of the closet, trying to look normal and unflustered. I think I'm doing an amazing job until I spot my reflection in a window and see that my hair is all over the place. Spencer has already gone, off to do the big scene. It's a closed set, and I can't really ask to watch without sounding like a pervert. Luckily there's something to distract me. My phone has started buzzing in my bag.

"Nish!"

"Hey."

I can't figure out her tone.

"Do you hate me?"

There's a beat as she thinks, and I brace myself.

"Yes, that is obviously what I was calling to say."

"I'm so sorry—we had this extra scene to shoot and then an early start the next day, and I forgot what day it was because I have the brain of an IDIOT. So Rosie got my chocolate thing?"

"Ha! Yeah, she did."

"Why 'ha'?"

"It said, 'I'm sorry in capitals.'"

"Yeah, I know; that's what I asked for!"

"No, as in, the message was *I'm sorry in capitals*. The whole thing. In lower case."

"Oh man!"

"On the plus side, she laughed, so I think she hates you less."

"Does she? I got a text from her, and it was nice, but I don't think she's ever sent a not-nice text in her life, so you can never be sure."

"What you said about coming back on your next day off, though—I think you should do that."

Nish is always right. I did promise to come back on my next day off. And then I had a day off yesterday and spent it with Spencer. Let's pretend that didn't happen.

"I have a day off on Friday."

I swallow the unreasonable voice that's telling me I have to be with Spencer all the time. He'll still be here if we're apart for the day.

Gabi has joined the conversation.

Gabi: Okay, so I have NEWS.

Nish: Drum roll . . .

Rosie: Oooh!

Mia: This reminds me of the time you said you had a surprise for me in your room, and when I opened my eyes you were mooning me.

Gabi: I've sort of gotten together with Spencer!

Gabi: You always bring that up, Mia, I think you liked it.

Gabi: ;)

Mia: That or I'm scarred. But hooray!

Nish: Have you slept with him?

Gabi: Nish, I am shocked!

Nish: You did, didn't you!

Gabi: Okay, yes. It was AMAZING. Wasn't it, Mia? Mia knows ;)

Nish: How?? Was she watching?

Mia: NO! She Facebooked me about it. In detail.

Rosie: Isn't it a little soon?

Gabi: We're getting on really well. He was shooting this scene and I had this great idea for what he should do in it (actually, I gave him loooooads of great ideas for it), and then he did them all and everybody's raving about him!

Nish: But he told them that you helped him, right?

Gabi: No, but I mean, I'm just the intern, aren't I? He's the actor man.

Nish: You should think about your career too.

Gabi: More excitement about my NEWS please!

Mia: ARGGHHHHHHHHHHH!

Rosie: Yaaaaaaaaaaaaaaay!

Gabi: Thank you, everyone. (Not you, Nish.) I'm going to meet his mom and brother!

Nish: Wow, you move fast!

Rosie: Yeah, sounds serious! What's going to happen when you finish the internship?

Gabi: Argh, sorry, got to go—have to take the lunch order.

Gabi: LOVE YOU BYE x

Gabi has left the conversation.

CHAPTER 31

There's a ramp going up to the door. It's the bottom apartment of a Victorian house, a bit like Spencer's. It's a little weird that he and his friends have the whole thing and his mother just has a floor. I assumed he came from a rich background to be living somewhere so nice. Spencer has his own key and lets us in.

It's all a little last minute, and I sort of invited myself. Spencer was supposed to be going to some industry party with other people his agent represents. He didn't sound very excited about it.

"Who wants to sit around talking to a bunch of reality TV stars?" he said.

"Yeah, sounds terrible," I replied, thinking, *ME. I do!*

Then he remembered he'd made other plans and told me he was supposed to go to his mom's for dinner.

I said, "That would be lovely," and he didn't uninvite me, so here I am.

A woman's voice calls "Spencer?" from a back room, and a blur rushes past me to stop beside Spencer. It turns out to be a small boy, who kicks him in the leg.

Spencer shouts, "Hey, Monkeyboy . . ." and grabs the boy by the back of his T-shirt as he tries to run away, and then tickles him. While he's doing that, a woman comes into the hallway using a crutch.

"My boy! And you must be Gabi. Come through, come through."

In the kitchen she gives me a kiss on the cheek. The boy comes bombing into the room again and slides across the kitchen floor, barely avoiding bashing into her crutch.

"Joel!" Spencer snaps.

"Oh, I'll get him back." His mom waves her hand dismissively and then points the end of the crutch at Joel. "Good for a swift crack on the shins, this thing," she says confidentially to me. "You should get one to keep him in check," she adds, nodding at Spencer.

Spencer's mom has MS. She tells me about it while Spencer takes over the cooking. He stands with his back to us as he chops some tomatoes on the kitchen counter. I can't see his face as his mom talks about the illness, and I think his shoulders look tense.

His mom is totally relaxed, though, as she arranges some cushions on a kitchen chair, sits, and leans back. She tells me to take a seat at the table.

"It's a bummer because they don't think I'm fit to work. I told them I used to manage this building—that the boys know me and will take turns carrying me when my legs are bad. No sense of humor!"

She says the pain comes and goes, and the last time she spoke to Spencer it was a bad time and she was complaining. He said he'd come over tonight because "he panics."

The whole way through we're interrupted by Joel, who's making George's Marvelous Medicine in a bucket because he's reading the book at school. He makes me promise to try some when he's finished, but I'm hoping he'll forget, because earlier he absentmindedly told us he was stirring the slugs in, before asking his mom if she had any yogurt she didn't want anymore.

Spencer's mom and I start talking about who we like most in soap operas, despite Spencer complaining that we're being ridiculous. She tells him not to be such an old fart, and then clinks her wineglass against mine.

I feel like I'm beginning to map out Spencer's life, and a clearer picture of him is coming into view.

I'm thrilled when she gets onto the subject of *The Halls*. When she found out Spencer had a line in it, she bought the first season boxed set and watched the whole thing.

"That Harry's something else, isn't he?" She nudges me.

"OH MY GOD, YES!" Definitely feeling a little bit tipsy now.

I can see Spencer is grinning as he drains the spaghetti and then when we tell him to hurry up, he comes obediently over with the food. I tell Spencer's mom spaghetti is my absolute favorite and she says, "Who knew?" and winks at Spencer. I finish my plate and the rest of Joel's too, because he's not looking too marvelous after his medicine, and then I get seconds.

Spencer's mom says she likes a girl who can eat. That

was also how I impressed Max's mom—with my appetite. I think I put on fourteen pounds just being in their house. But it was fourteen pounds that included lots of yummy cakes, so totally worth it.

Spencer's mom is constantly embarrassing him, so I can see where he gets his sense of humor. She tells me she was very excited to hear I was coming over, because she doesn't usually get to meet the girlfriends.

"Um, she's not my girlfriend. She's just some girl who keeps following me around. I can't shake her off," says Spencer.

"Oh, don't be like that, *babe*," I reply. Our eyes meet, and I see him trying to fight off his smile.

After dinner, his mom takes out a photo album, and I discover that Spencer went through a stage when he was about six of wearing only a bow tie. His entire childhood keeps us entertained for hours, stopping only when Joel demands I sing "Happy Birthday" to him, even though it's not his birthday. Then he asks me to sing the dead cat song. I tell him I don't know the words, but I can join in soon, because the words are apparently "Dead cat, dead cat," over and over. When he says he's going to get the cat to join in too, I give Spencer a look of fear, which puts him in hysterics. Thankfully the cat Joel comes back with is very much alive and surprisingly tolerant about being dragged around the kitchen by a five-year-old. Spencer intervenes only at the point when we hear Joel say, "Tilly wants medicine."

I ask to see Spencer's bedroom and he says, "Steady on," which sets his mom off cackling. I try to say that I'm just nosy about his life, not suggesting anything, but they aren't having any of it.

I get a flashback of Max's dad glaring at me whenever I went anywhere near Max's bedroom.

Spencer does give me a tour, though. His bedroom is just the storage room because they moved here after his mom was diagnosed, which was only a few years ago. I think of the man in the photo album who's there in all of Spencer's photos. I probably shouldn't ask about him, but I do, because the question is hanging in the air. And because I've had two glasses of wine.

He looks at his feet and then up at me. And then he talks. Their dad freaked out over the whole MS thing, and then it turned out he was having an affair with his boss. He lives with her now in this big house with her kids, who are Joel's age. Spencer's mom won't take any money from his dad, but he pays Spencer guilt money that he uses for rent. He bites the inside of his cheek.

"Once they pay me my first big acting check . . ." He pauses, giving me a look as if to add, *which I know sounds ridiculous.* ". . . then I'm buying her a house."

On the Underground back, Spencer puts his arm around me. "Thank you for coming."

"It's fine," I tell him. "I get paid for this, right?"

He doesn't seem to hear that and keeps on talking. Sometimes I think he doesn't appreciate my comedy gold. And he also doesn't seem to appreciate that I had an absolute blast at his house. I love hanging out with people's families. When I knew I had to break up with Max, one of the things holding me back was that I wouldn't be able to hang out at his house anymore. I was always texting his mom. His dad, not so much, because of the time he told Max that going out with me might hold him back in life.

"When are you going back home again?" says Spencer.

"Tomorrow."

"I could come with you."

"OKAY!"

He pretends to wince at how loud my voice is, but then he smiles.

Thinking about it, I should probably have shrugged and said something more cool like, "Yeah, come, or don't. *Whatever.*"

But I didn't.

CHAPTER 32

I did text telling him the train time. He replied saying,
`I've got an interview!` Which was nice, but irrelevant. He's got a minute to arrive or he's going to miss it. I
hover near the turnstile, watching the escalator that comes
up from the Underground. Should I just get on the train?
He's got only thirty seconds now. And there's the guard's
whistle. I'm going to have to just go. I run across the platform and leap onto the train. I'm there. And the doors stay
open. A few people look up from their seats as I catch my
breath. I so need to get more exercise. Or any exercise.

I look up and see Spencer is behind me, casually strolling up the platform. And just before he gets to the door he
does an impression of me running. In my head I thought it
was a swift, elegant sprint, a bit like Usain Bolt; according
to Spencer's impression, it was Usain Bolt with no control
over his limbs or face.

On the train he keeps yawning. It turns out he went to the party last night. Apparently his agent called him up and forced him to go. I'd like to just casually drop into the conversation, "Why didn't you invite me?" but I think it goes against my "trying not to seem too eager" plan. There is the danger I'll just blurt it out the next time I'm annoyed, though.

Then Spencer moves to the seat next to me and kisses me and strangely I forget about it, along with all the other thoughts I've ever had.

They're in the usual spot in the parking lot. I see the manic waving as soon as we walk through the entrance. There's a slight pause and a moment when they turn to each other, which must be them realizing I've brought Spencer with me. A few yards from them, I start running. I aim straight at Nish and attack her with a huge kiss on the cheek. She pushes me off.

No Max, thank God, but there are a few other people from school. There is a little awkward silence as we get settled down.

Then I do the introductions, obviously not including Nish and Rosie, whom Spencer has already met. And I show him a picture of Mia on my phone and prop her up against a lemonade bottle.

"So how's all the shooting going?" Nish says, while Rosie looks at her phone.

"Yeah, it's—" Spencer's phone starts ringing. "Oh, I need to take this. Sorry, Nadia, I'll be back in one sec."

"It's Nish," she snaps.

He's on the phone forever. Everyone smiles politely and carries on the conversation, but I keep looking over at him, wondering when he's planning on coming back over.

I pick up pretend Mia from the lemonade bottle and text actual Mia.

THIS IS AWFUL. THEY HATE HIM :(

She replies in a few minutes. I love Mia.

I'm sure it's not that bad. You all hated Jamie at first. It will be fine, don't worry! x

She's right. For the first few times Jamie came out with us as Mia's boyfriend, I would only glare at him, and make deliberate comments about how lovely Dan, Mia's ex, was. Then he bought me some shoes after hearing me go on about how much I wanted them. So I said I hoped he didn't think shoes would make me think he was a nice person (although I did keep them). I only really started liking him when we were in New Zealand and Mia was telling me what he's like when he's with her.

I reply.

He got Nish's name wrong!!

And so does Mia.

I hope he's made out his will. x

While I'm chatting I have my phone in my hand and I fire off a quick text to let Mom know that I'm back for the day. I'm sure we could fit in a visit to the house before we have to get the train back. She replies immediately as well. I do have them all well trained.

GREAT PERHAPS NOT AT THE HOUSE YOUR
DAD IS NOT WELL I CAN COME OUT AND
MEET YOU FOR COFFEE SORRY CANNOT TURN
OFF CAPS LOVE MUM ZZ

Spencer is over by a tree, still talking on the phone. Then Rosie says she's going to use the bathroom in the café. So I jump up as well; it's a good opportunity to check whether she has definitely forgiven me.

As she sees me get up, she smiles. So I give her a big hug and say, "You love me again, don't you?"

She says, "Yumf," because her head is trapped in my boobs. She frees herself. "Of course; it was fine. I just wanted you to be there! And you've got your *exciting* summer hanging with the celebs! I'm so happy for you, after the year you had."

"It has been SO COOL." I jump in quickly. "Especially since it's turning into a summer of lurve!"

Rosie doesn't say anything.

"What?" I say, even though I know I shouldn't push it.

"Don't you think it's . . . a bit . . . insensitive?"

The guilt is like a dead weight in my stomach.

"Max has been doing really well," Rosie goes on. "I think he'd be really upset if he knew you'd brought Spencer here."

I swallow. What I should say is, "I know. I haven't been thinking about Max. Because it hurts to think about Max. And so I pretend there is nothing to think about."

What I do say is, "Why the *hell* are you contacting Max? You're supposed to be *my* friend."

She looks really shocked. "Look, I wasn't sure how to tell you . . ."

"I don't want to hear it!"

She blinks and looks as though she might cry. Again, no tears from me. Because I am clearly heartless. We get to the café, do our thing, and come walking back really quickly, not saying a word. Just as Spencer walks over.

I practically jump on him to get away from Rosie.

"Spencer! My mom's coming out for coffee! You'll love her—well, she's a little weird, but it'll be fun!"

"Ah." Spencer's mouth twists to the side. "I've got to head back, actually. I just did an interview for this online magazine thing over the phone. And I don't have any photos they can use with it, so . . ."

"Can't you do it tomorrow?" I can feel everyone at the picnic watching us.

"No . . . Not really. They want to put the interview online ASAP."

Each word jabs at me, but I try to keep calm.

He shifts from foot to foot and then gestures toward the park entrance where we came in. "So I better . . ."

I get a flash of annoyance and the words come out before I can stop them. "Why didn't you invite me to the party last night?" I snap.

He laughs in an awkward, shocked kind of way and

steers me away from the group so we're over on our own. I've definitely pushed it too far.

"Look, I'm sorry, but my agent is going to get me an audition for an ad campaign. If I get it, that's six grand. I kind of want to show her that I'm prepared to make the effort. And the party was a work thing."

I insist on walking him back to the station even though I'm sure he can find his own way. I want to avoid the questions from everyone about what we're arguing about. Nish's eyes flash daggers at me when I tell her we're leaving. We've only been here twenty minutes. I tell her I'll come back, but even as I'm saying it I'm thinking that I'll get Mom to meet me earlier.

Spencer doesn't say anything. He goes to take my hand and I move it away.

"Don't be silly about this!" he says.

"I'm not!"

I see him raise an eyebrow, and a horrible thought strikes me. There's nothing forcing him to stay with me. If I get bitchy, he could just decide he doesn't want to do this anymore.

We're almost at the station now, and he takes my hand again. He stops and pulls me into him and kisses me.

"Come on, grump," he says.

I break into a smile as a warm, tingly feeling floats down from my chest to my stomach.

And then a figure behind him comes into focus.

It's Max.

CHAPTER 33

Max stands rooted to the spot just outside the station entrance and Spencer sets off toward him, turning back when he realizes I've pulled my hand away.

Then Max's mom appears. She's just gotten tickets from the machine outside the station and comes over to hand him one. She turns around to see what Max is looking at.

"Gabi!" she says, a bit too brightly.

Spencer looks from me to Max; he has no idea what's going on.

Max looks different. He's wearing a more tight-fitting T-shirt than usual, and his jeans aren't as low-slung. But he still hitches them up, the way he does when he's nervous. He's looking at Spencer now, as if he's taking in every detail. Spencer looks so relaxed. And confident. And older. My heart goes out to Max, and I can't do anything. I take a step forward and see the way his mom is looking at me. It's a look of absolute death.

"How are you?" I say, way too cheerfully.

"Um, I . . ." Max's voice wobbles. He stops and turns bright red, and then breathes in to try again.

"Excellent!" his mom cuts in. "I'm sure you've heard we've got him back into Leeds. Just heading up there now to figure out the accommodation." She's beaming at me, but the look of death is still twinkling in her eyes.

"Right . . . ," Spencer says, turning to me. "I'd better go."

"Okay." I nod.

"Bye," he says and turns back toward the station. He nods at Max and says, "All right, man," and then he's almost at the entrance.

I wave, but a bit too vigorously, and my ring flies off my hand and bounces on the sidewalk. Both Spencer and Max step toward it. Max hesitates, but then carries on determinedly. Spencer puts his hands up and hangs back.

Max comes over, holding out the ring.

"Here you go," he says in a low voice.

"It's Granny's!" I tell him. "It's really old and precious."

"Then you probably shouldn't throw it on the ground," he says, smiling a little.

He shuffles off, hitching up his jeans. I always used to give him wedgies, just to point out how much boxer there was on show. That probably wouldn't be appropriate now.

Just then the train pulls in and everyone snaps out of the awkward moment, because they need to get onto the platform. Spencer waves, and I watch him go off to the opposite end of the train from Max and his mom.

Then they're both gone. And I'm on my own. Which I never am, if I can help it. Nobody who knows me would know, but when I'm on my own I think too much. If it's silent when I'm with someone, I'll fill the space by saying tons of stupid stuff. But I can't do that when I'm alone. Passersby would think I was insane. I get out my phone to push away all the thoughts creeping in. I text Mia.

OMG. Spencer and Max met. SO
AWKWARD!!!

She calls me.
"Are you okay?"
I shake my head and sniff. I've got that stupid rock in my throat again and can't speak. But she just stays on the phone and waits till I can talk.
I tell her how being with Spencer can make me go from being excited to uncertain in the space of a moment.
I hang up when I see my mom across the road, coming to meet me for coffee, and realize I got a text while I was on the phone.

Sorry about today. When's your next
day off? I have a treat planned.
Spencer x

CHAPTER 34

Johnny Green is there when I'm waiting outside one of the offices at the studio to meet the editor and the writer the next day. He has his head bent down, looking at his phone, and his amazing sweepy bangs are falling over his face. Even though I'm much more into Bad Boy Hugh these days, it would still be cool if Johnny Green was my famous friend. I have only a few days left of the internship, so time is running out to make celebrity pals. And I'd kind of forgotten that the people here are famous. I'm more excited to be meeting the writers. It could be my chance to make them really remember me. When Johnny glances up, I try flashing him a smile, but he just frowns and then slouches off, his eyes glued to his phone again. I don't think we'll be staying in touch.

There are noises behind the door. They must be ready to see me. Maybe I should admit I'm not very good at spelling?

I've brought my notebook with the thing I was writing that is probably awful. The door opens and a friendly face appears. Her name is Emily, and she's the writer. The editor is Hazel. I was expecting scary old people, but they both look like they're in their midtwenties.

"Come in!" she says. The office looks really cozy. There's a wall of half-naked men posters, which I definitely approve of, and dotted around one of the computers—a swanky-looking Mac—are an assortment of plastic and porcelain ducks.

"They bring me luck," says Emily. "Well, except when I'm pulling an all-nighter and I start talking to them."

"Like the recent last-minute rewrites!" mutters Hazel. She clears some papers off a sofa.

"I'm not very good at spelling," I say as I sit down.

They look at each other and shrug.

"We find the best starting point is talking," says Emily.

"And tea," adds Hazel.

"So all the writers sit down and talk about what we want from this season," Emily continues, showing me a big sheet of paper with lots of scribbles and arrows and crossings out on it. "What worked well in the last season, what sort of journeys we want the characters to go on, so we can structure the season into episodes, which we then go off and write."

She says that she shows the scenes to Hazel as she writes them, and together they make sure that the structure works for a thirty-minute episode, as well as tying in with the characters' story lines for the season. And then they go over the dialogue to make sure it fits exactly with how the characters speak.

Then they show me examples of scenes in which the dialogue is "too exposition-y" and how they would change it.

I am hugely excited to discover that Emily has written tons of the scenes featuring Tom and Priya, and I tell her that they were my favorite couple in the first season. She's delighted and says that they wanted to make it so that the audience would be desperate for them to get back together by the time it happens in season two. Then Hazel nudges her, because it's clear from my face that I don't know what happens in the finale. Everyone's being really cagey about it. I tell Hazel and Emily that they have my solemn vow of secrecy, although I don't tell then my solemn vow of secrecy doesn't include Mia and Max. Well, just Mia now.

I take a deep breath and summon the courage to turn to the page of my notebook that has my idea on it. It's a story about a boy band whose members all go to school together, and then they hit the big time and girls everywhere go crazy for them. My main thought initially when I was writing it was that I could hold the auditions for the boy band members. But then I started thinking it could be really good; the band could have actual songs that people could download. Max was going to write the raps.

Hazel and Emily are really nice about it, and we brainstorm some ideas for scenes and bits of dialogue, getting me to think about what I would put in a pilot episode.

Without my noticing, I've been there for two hours, and I suddenly realize I need to get back to actual work. I practically skip out into the hall, absolutely buzzing with how fun and exciting that was. I'm definitely bringing in cookies to say thank you to Hazel and Emily.

Spencer is lurking in the corridor outside their office. I didn't think I was seeing him until later, when he has our treat planned.

"Hey," he says, grinning and holding out his phone with a web page loaded. "My interview's up!"

Talent spotted!

We've caught up with *The Halls'* hot new hunk, bad boy Hugh St. Clair, played by sexy Spencer Black.

Name: Spencer Edward Black
Age: 20
Lives: In Clapham with some friends—I have one year left at college, so that's one more year of a party house!

How does it feel to be *The Halls'* new resident hottie?
I'm not gonna lie—it's awesome! Before this my biggest fan was my mom, so it' great to know there will be a few more people watching me now!

Will you and Johnny Green be performing a battle of the haircuts?
Do you think I can compete with those bangs? But seriously, Johnny better up his game. He's got competition now!

Can you tell us a bit about Hugh St. Clair?
Hugh is rich, brooding, and—so it says in my script—dangerously attractive. He's at NLU on false pretenses, after being expelled from his school for reasons that will become clear. He's on a self-destructive path and out to cause trouble for the other students.

Rumor has it you've been filming some steamy scenes with *Halls* geek-turned-hottie Jas (aka Heidi Adams)— any romance of the real-life sort blossoming there?
Oh, I couldn't possibly comment . . .

Does that mean you can make our day and tell us that you're still available?
Both my character and I are young, free, and single. Hugh is trying to avoid getting tied down and have as much fun as possible, whereas I'm keeping a lookout for Ms. Right.

Click <u>here</u> to go to *The Halls'* YouTube channel, where you can watch episode one of Spencer's exclusive Behind the Scenes video blogs.

CHAPTER 35

Oh, I couldn't possibly comment . . .

I shouldn't bring it up. I know I shouldn't. It's just stayed in my brain since I saw it yesterday. I signed up for e-mail alerts featuring Spencer Black as well, so I've been sent more articles saying how great it is that sexy Spence is single. Spencer's already said that his agent told him what to say. She wants to create a buzz around him, so he needs to be "single with a whiff of possible romance," apparently.

And what would he say, anyway? "Actually, I've been meeting a girl in a closet recently, and she came over and had spaghetti with my mom"? Although I would have preferred it if he had said that.

I could change my Facebook status to "In a Relationship" and see what he does . . . An imaginary Mia pops into my head at that point and says "NO." And I know I can't do that, because Max might see. We're still friends on there because neither of us wanted to unfriend the other. We've both changed our profile picture from that black-and-white one of us kissing as if we didn't know the camera was there—which took about twenty tries to get right.

I could just ask Spencer. Casually drop it in. *So, young, free, and single and on the lookout for Ms. Right, ARE WE?*

I turn and look at him from the side, with the shimmering water behind him. I just can't figure him out at all. He's chewing his lip and frowning slightly. Does that mean he's enjoying this and thinks we're an item? Or is he wondering where Ms. Right might be hiding? Or is he hungry?

I need to turn off my brain and enjoy the treat. Spencer booked us tickets on the waterbus from Little Venice to Camden, and it's lovely floating past all the trees and under the little bridges. Or it would be, if I could chill the hell out. I don't even really look at the London Zoo when we go past that. Mia would be ashamed.

When we get to Camden, Spencer wants to go to a pub. I'm about to tell him he'll need to sneak me in, but then I think I don't want to remind him of my age. I try to go in subtly instead, but Spencer asks me why I'm creeping like a cartoon burglar. I just tell him I have a cramp.

We sit on a sofa, hidden away in the corner of the pub, and Spencer puts his arm around me, pulling me toward him. We kiss, and his hands are on my waist. He moves his thumb back and forth over my hip and the waistband of my jeans. Despite the thoughts buzzing around my brain, I get a surge so strong it almost makes me shiver, and I press myself closer to him. He draws his head back so our foreheads are touching and says, "Are you coming back to my place?"

Getting back from Spencer's takes extra long because the trains are delayed. I told myself it would be fine to go back with him as long as I wasn't late getting home. But we got carried away, and I couldn't text Granny because my phone died on the boat trip. I'm hoping she won't have noticed. She's been a bit crazy lately, and will probably be off wind-surfing or mud wrestling or something like that.

I'm distracted by that thought as I walk into the house and so at first I don't notice that Granny is sitting on a chair directly facing the door watching me. With a drop-dead gorgeous Spanish man.

"Where the HELL have you been?" she rages.

"Out with Spencer!"

She looks like she would run over and throttle me if the man wasn't there. He looks very awkward and then edges over and offers me his hand.

"Hello," he says in a lovely husky accent. "I am Alejandro. Please to meet you, Gabi."

"Are you my new grandpa?" I say, half in fear and half in a swoon because I'm holding his hand.

"Ah, no—I am a gay."

"Alejandro has one of those gay marriages," says Granny, as if that's something fancy. And then she remembers that she's supposed to be angry with me and starts shouting again. She said she called Alejandro over because she had no idea where I was and my phone was off and she was worried sick.

Alejandro backs away toward the kitchen and starts rummaging through cupboards. My fingers are crossed that he's making some food. I turn to Granny.

"I thought you were cool with me doing whatever. You haven't seemed to be paying much attention."

"I may . . ." She stops. There are tears in her eyes. "I may have been a bit manic lately, but I've certainly been keeping an eye on you." She looks at me, her eyes shining. "Everything else is just distraction. He's left a bloody hole in my life, that man. I need to keep busy, or . . ." She swallows.

I throw my arms around her, feeling hot tears seeping onto my cheeks. She strokes my hair.

"You make sure you take care of yourself—promise me?" she says.

As Mom steered me outside, I heard Granny saying, "Oh, love, it's fine. It's been tough on her." I looked back at her, and she gave me a big smile. Then the whole room lurched and I tripped. I heard my aunt Kath tut.

I couldn't even remember all the speeches people made when we got back to Granny's after Grandpa's funeral. The part in the crematorium was really short anyway. But the image of the crappy cardboard coffin sitting on the conveyor belt won't go away. It suddenly stopped when the coffin was halfway through the hole and a man had to come and fiddle with it to get it going again.

Granny said, "He always was a stubborn bastard." But her voice cracked in the middle. I put my hand on hers, and Max put his on mine.

As soon as we got to her place, I started helping myself to drinks, rolling my eyes at Mom when she told me to slow down.

Granny wanted readings and speeches at the wake, so we could share all our memories of Grandpa in the house he loved. With everyone around eating and drinking, it could almost have been a family Christmas.

When it was my turn to read, I looked down and the words on the paper swirled around and made no sense. Max was behind me, and he leaned over and read the first line.

"Let me not to the marriage of true minds admit impediments."

After that I could read it. I'd learned it by heart the night before, and all the words came back.

I was sitting outside on the stoop afterward to get some air. Then someone sat down beside me. Max.

I felt hollow and I wanted him to leave.

"I brought you some water," he said.

"I'm fine."

"You should drink it."

"Max, can you just go?"

He put the glass down. "No."

The sound of the glass on the patio seemed to cut through all the cloudiness. Thoughts I'd been trying not to think were suddenly clear and sharp and unavoidable. Everyone thought it was stupid that we were getting married, but they'd stopped saying it because Grandpa dying and the stuff with Dad was so horrible and real. They were hoping my silly, pretend engagement would keep me happy. So now they were acting like it was great.

"Everyone's laughing at us behind our backs," I said slowly. "We're a joke."

"But we're not a joke. We know that. That's what matters."

"Then they're laughing at me, Max. They think everything I do is ridiculous, and they go along with it because they feel sorry for me."

"I'm not laughing at you, Gabi. I know you."

I finally looked at him. "I hate that you know me so well." Then I shoved him, and he nearly fell off the step. "What's wrong with you? Why don't you leave? I'm clearly insane."

He looked up at the window of the house. I must have been shouting. Then he looked back at me, and I saw it in his eyes. Sympathy. He felt sorry for me too. That was when the cold, numb feeling started.

I shoved him in the chest again. "Why do you put up with this?"

He breathed out slowly and put his chin on his hands. "I'm not going anywhere."

CHAPTER 36

I can't believe it's my last day. The last couple of weeks have flown by. It's probably because work has been nonstop. They've been filming five or six scenes a day, so there's always a prop to find or a mess to clean up. I've become well known by some of the local taxi drivers because of the rides I've arranged to shuttle actors between the studio and the university. And once because a couple of them wandered off and got lost.

Every spare moment I've spent with Spencer. It's helping me to not think about the fact that I haven't spoken to Rosie or Nish since I snapped at Rosie. Mia asked me what was going on, but I ignored that part of her message.

Spencer's been taking me on more treats. The other night we went for a walk in Regent's Park in the evening. And the one before that we went back to the Moroccan place in Camden. His Behind the Scenes YouTube videos have been getting tons of hits, so I know he's really happy, even though he likes to pretend he thinks it's all ridiculous.

Every time I'm with him I feel excited, as if I don't know where the night is going to go. And when I look over at him at work, I love that we're sharing a secret sort of life. We can't tell anyone at work, because Sexy Spence is supposed to be young, free, and single. Well, we aren't *supposed* to tell anyone—but I may have told my friend Dave the janitor.

We haven't talked about what happens when I go back to school. But then, we haven't said we're going to end things either. Spencer's booked this fancy hotel tomorrow for my last night in London. I guess we'll talk about it then.

It's like the show knew I'd be leaving today as well, because they're shooting two scenes from the last episode—the finale scenes for Tom and Priya and for Harry and Jas. From the bits and pieces I've heard around the set, I've mostly been able to piece together what happens. Jude—the girl Tom got pregnant—has been making Priya think that they're a couple. Priya finally accepted that she and Tom were over and went to buy a onesie that says "My Daddy Is Awesome." In the finale, Tom is waiting on a bench, thinking he's going to meet Jude to talk about prenatal classes, but Jude went to see Priya to tell her the truth—that Tom still loves Priya. So it's Priya who arrives to meet Tom on the bench. She gives him the onesie and then they kiss. Or at least I hope they do.

Harry and Jas's story line goes that Jas ended up getting kidnapped by some drug dealers who were after Hugh, and Harry rescued her. Walking back across the campus, they hold hands (which is *huge*, because the whole way through Harry has always refused to do anything that makes him look like her boyfriend). Back in their room, Jas goes to take a shower, and Harry gets something out of his pocket and looks at it—a small box, just the right size for an engagement ring. But then he sees Jen, his ex, standing there.

I don't know if I can actually deal with this much excitement. But I manage to hold it together, only letting out the odd squeak while getting everyone their coffee as usual.

The last scene I watch is actually one of Spencer smoking a cigarette under a tree, then dropping it, putting it out with his foot, and staring moodily into the distance. When Mark yells "Cut!" I applaud. Then I remember that for everyone else, filming is not over.

Nina, the location manager, gives me a card signed by everyone and says that I can go for pizza with a group of the cast and crew. Everyone mostly gets along really well, no matter what job they do, and there are only a few actors who don't mix with everyone else. I want to go and grab Spencer's hand and tell everyone about us. He's busy, though, filming a Behind the Scenes party video. So I tell Nina I'll come along and that I'll be with Spencer and that he's my sort-of boyfriend.

She looks surprised. "I thought he was with—" But

then she's interrupted by a phone call. She was clearly going to say Heidi, so I'm glad I put her straight.

I head back to the studio, where Spencer is in the middle of filming the blog with Heidi. They are doing a Kiss, Marry, Avoid thing with pictures of other members of the cast.

When Heidi says she'd kiss Spencer's character I crumple the side of my good-bye card, but I don't react other than that. When Spencer says he'd marry Heidi's character and gives her a flirty glance, I shout, "WTF!" (except obviously I don't say it in letters) and everyone turns around.

There's a moment of complete silence.

"Um, we'll probably have to shoot that part again," says Spencer.

They all go back to what they're doing and forget about me.

When Spencer finishes, he comes over. He looks a little annoyed.

"Well, that was a special moment," he says.

"I'm sorry—it slipped out. I didn't like seeing her all over you like a . . . slug."

His frown breaks then, and he laughs. "It's just to generate a bit of excitement about our story line." He puts his arms around my shoulders and gives me a squeeze.

"I've been invited out for pizza with everyone," I say through a squashed mouth.

"Oh yeah?" He lets me go and reaches for the phone I've just felt vibrate in his pocket. "I'm going to dinner with some of the guys."

"Surely that's the same thing I'm going to?" I ask.

"I don't think so. It's just a small group of us."

There's a pause. And a flicker of something I can't read in Spencer's eyes.

"You can come along if you want."

CHAPTER 37

I reach for an olive at the same time as someone else and we bash hands. It's Johnny Green. He's sitting on the other side of Ben Hart, who's next to me. I've discovered that he uses the fact that he plays a gay character on the show to chat up women. I heard some of the waitresses talking about how sweet he was when I was washing my hands in the bathroom earlier. But from the way he kept miming groping them and then winking at Spencer, I would say he's definitely more of a sex offender than a sweetheart.

I decide to try talking to Johnny Green again while we both have our hands in the olives.

"What did you order, Johnny?"

He frowns at me and looks confused. His eyes are glazed over, and he keeps blinking a lot. It turns out he does a lot of drugs and is usually out of his mind on something. He

203

doesn't answer me because he's suddenly fascinated by how shiny his fork is.

Well, this is fun.

On the other side of the table, Spencer, Heidi, Heidi's dad, and Spencer's agent are all deep in conversation. We are clearly going to completely miss drinks with all the others after their pizza.

I go over and sit at the bar for a while and tell the waitresses what a creep Ben Hart is. They decide they're going to play up to it so that they get a big tip out of him. Then Heidi's dad walks past me on the phone. He's speaking in a low voice, but I think I catch something like, "They'll be coming out at eight."

I get a tap on the shoulder. Spencer. Suddenly my evening is looking up. He beckons me into a corner where we can't be seen.

About an hour later—half spent in the corner with Spencer and half in the bar, where Ben letches, Johnny Green stares blankly, and Heidi keeps touching Spencer's leg—everyone leaves to go to some exclusive club in the West End, but I have to get home because Granny has me on a strict curfew at the moment. The waitresses see me standing next to Spencer by the door and one of them really unsubtly mouths "Is that him?" because during my conversation about Ben with them I might have accidentally let it slip that Spencer is my secret boyfriend. I give her wide eyes, but I nod. I think Spencer notices, but he doesn't say anything. I walk alongside him as we go through the gates to where the taxis are. Then I grab his hand to say good-bye just as there's a lot of shouting and camera flashes going off.

Most of the paparazzi are calling for Heidi, Ben, and Johnny, but I hear one of them shout to Spencer. He pulls his hand away from mine and turns away from me, shielding his face with his hand, as he gets in a taxi.

In all the confusion, we don't even get to say good-bye properly.

One of the photographers is standing next to me. It's a bit calmer now that most of the cast has gone. "Who are you, then?" he asks gruffly.

"Oh, I'm just a runner."

"That fun, is it?"

"Oh my God, it's awesome. Well, I'm totally obsessed with *The Halls* and everyone in it anyway, but working there is amazing."

"You friends with any of them?" He's fiddling with his camera, but looks up and smiles at me. He's got a round, friendly face a bit like my dad's.

"Yeah, Jen is really nice in real life. And Spencer Black . . . he's my sort-of boyfriend."

I should probably stop telling people that.

CHAPTER 38

Spencer is in a suit. I ask him if he's celebrating the adver-
tisement money coming through, and he says, "I haven't
shot the commercial yet!" like that was a stupid thing to
say, which I suppose it was. He tells me he got some more
guilt money out of his dad.

He meets me in the lobby and takes me to the reception
desk. The hotel is *enormous*. My heels make a noise like
horses' hooves on the marble stairs. I'm wearing my little
black dress, which I wear for anything fancy, although it
must be about a tenth of the price of Spencer's suit. I suddenly remember it's the dress I wore in Paris with Max.

I give over my bag at the desk, and they say someone
will take it up to our room.

"It's like being a grown-up!" I whisper to Spencer as we
head toward the restaurant.

"I am a grown-up," he replies.

"All right, douche!"

He laughs.

The restaurant part seems really silent. I guess it's because it's so big that none of the tables are very near to each other. It's really fancy, but in a completely different way from Radleigh Castle. It's all done in 1920s style, and there's a huge chandelier in the middle of the ceiling with glittering gems hanging from it.

Spencer seems distracted. Before we order he goes off to take a phone call from his agent, leaving me absolutely starving. I look longingly at the wait staff as they go past in the hope that they will take pity on me and give me some more free bread.

One of them does—a smiley waitress named Flo. She brings me some butter as well and I tell her that I love her, just as Spencer comes back.

He raises his eyebrows. "I knew if I left you alone, you'd go off with a waitress!"

He's more relaxed now, and we sit there chatting. It feels like we're in our own little bubble. Then Flo comes over with the appetizers and Spencer has his elbow where she needs to put the plate on the table. I give him a nudge and he moves it, but he doesn't look up at her or say thank you when she puts the food down; he just carries on talking.

"Spencer!"

"What?" He looks up, shocked.

"You didn't say thank you!"

"Okay . . ."

"It's rude." I wave my hand to help make my point—and knock over my glass of water. The water runs all over the table, down toward Spencer's side, and then drips onto his pants. He jumps up.

"For fuck's sake! What's wrong with you? It's embarrassing taking you out."

I stare at him, open-mouthed. That came from nowhere. I have two options, really: the mature thing, which is to stand up and leave, or to throw my wine at him.

Actually, I do both.

I storm off toward the elevators. It's really hard to storm when you then have to wait for the elevator to arrive. I keep pushing the button, willing it to get there before Spencer catches up with me. He appears around the corner, and it occurs to me that I don't know where our room is or have the key.

By the time the elevator doors open, Spencer is standing next to me. I talk with my eyes straight ahead, determined not to look at him.

"Can I have the key, please?"

"Look, Gabi—"

"Actually, you can come with me and let me into the room. But don't talk to me."

We stand in the elevator, and he presses the button.

"Gabi, I snapped. I was in a bad mood."

"You seemed in a good mood when you got off the phone with your agent, actually."

"Well, I mean, I had lots of stuff to think about. Really important stuff."

The inside of the elevator doors is mirrored, so despite my efforts I'm looking right at Spencer. He looks flushed, and there's still an angry glint in his eye, possibly because he's thinking about his expensive new suit that is now covered in red wine.

We both stare at each other in silence as the back elevator doors open behind us. It's this weird intense stare, as if we don't know whether to continue arguing or make up. I turn to leave a moment before he does and I collide with him. As my hand brushes his, energy rushes through me, and suddenly my skin feels like it's on fire. Spencer looks at me, his mouth slightly open and his eyes sparkling, as if he felt it too. We move together and kiss. It's one deep, hard kiss without a breath that makes me feel almost as though I could get lost in him. It feels like an effort to break the spell and move apart. Then the elevator doors start to close, and Spencer puts his hand out to stop them.

Before I know it, we're in our expensive room. His hand slides up my leg under my dress, and I gasp as his fingers brush against me. I turn my head to the side and he kisses my neck as his fingers rub softly at first and then firmer.

My eyes are closed and then a moan escapes me and I open them. For some unknown reason, as the hotel room comes into focus, the thought appears in my brain that if it were Max and I staying in a hotel, the first thing we would have done is make a pile of free stuff from the room on the bed.

And I start laughing.

Spencer's hand freezes. He moves it away and then looks at me, his other hand still pressed to the wall above me. He looks a little freaked out, and waits for an explanation.

I'm still throbbing with desire, but also panic and that urge to laugh.

"Sorry . . . I don't know what's wrong with me."

"No . . . ," he says slowly. "I'm not totally sure either."

"It's just . . . it's a risk, isn't it? Every little thing is a risk, and I could go for it and you could turn out to be a psychopath, and it's really weird because with most things I do just go for it and don't think, and now—"

"Gabi," he says softly. "It's fine. Just . . . chill. Take as long as you want to decide whether I'm a psychopath."

"It's just that this is all new, and I thought I'd be cool with that, but I'm not. I'm nuts."

His mouth twists into a smile. "Well, just so you know, I'd prefer to be with you, nuts, than anyone else, sane."

He kisses me, gently now, understanding a little more. "Shall we watch movies in our pajamas and drink free tea?"

CHAPTER 39

I have no idea where I am. All the shapes in the room are strange and don't make sense. Slowly my eyes adjust to the darkness. White hotel sheets. Spencer. I peer over the side of the bed. White floor with a dark shape on it. It looks like a dead bird. A huge dead bird. One of those black beaky ones, like a raven or a crow. Are they different?

"Spencer," I whisper.

He grunts and rolls to the side.

"Spencer!"

"What?" His voice is muffled and sleepy.

"There's a dead bird on the floor."

"No, there isn't."

"There is. There definitely is. Can you take it out?"

He rolls onto his front with his face on the pillow. "What are you talking about?"

"Spencer, there's a dead bird on the floor, and if you don't help me get rid of it, then I'm going home. It's disgus— Oh no, wait. It's just my bra."

Now everything makes a lot more sense.

Spencer raises his head from the pillow. "You thought your bra was a dead bird."

"I thought I saw a beak."

He puts his forehead down on the pillow again. In despair, I think. Then I realize he's laughing.

He looks up at me. I'm sitting up, poised in what I must have thought was a good position for dead-bird watching. He holds his arm out to me. I can't really see his face in the half light, but I know he's smiling and his eyes are sparkling.

I slide down and fit into the crook of his body. He puts his arm around me and clasps his hand over mine. He leans over and whispers in my ear. "I love you a little bit, Gabi."

It takes all my effort not to leap out of the bed and jump up and down. But I just smile a huge, wide smile that he can't see and squeeze his hand.

"Good."

When I wake up he's gone, but there's a note.

Have gone to get you flowers, chocolates, and bacon bagels to apologize for being a dick. Would be lovely if you wanted to hang out all day with me.
Your friendly neighborhood psychopath,
Spencer x

I can't stop grinning. I want to call Mia and tell her everything. I jump off the bed and do a crazy dance over to my bag to get my phone. Ooh, I have an e-mail alert.

Alert: New article on Spencer Black
Scandal, sex appeal, stalkers: Spencer's got it all
Halls hottie Spencer Black, as well as getting the Pop-Goss team in a fluster, is causing a stir on set as well. Rumored to be dating his costar Heidi Adams after they shared some steamy scenes (click <u>here</u> to watch a sneak preview trailer of *The Halls* season 2!), Spencer was pictured hand in hand with a mystery lady at a cast outing. But is the picture all it appears? An insider informs us that Sexy Spence may just have attracted his very first obsessive fan.

"That's Gabi Morgan. She's an intern on the show who's got a major crush on Spencer," says our source. "She follows him everywhere and basically won't leave him alone. He found it flattering at first, but he's starting to get annoyed, to say the least—it's really affecting how things are going with Heidi."

And it could be more worrying than just a celeb crush. The girl openly admitted to our photographer that she's "obsessed with *The Halls* and everyone in it" and referred to Spencer as her "sort-of boyfriend."

"There are rumors circulating among the cast," our source tells us, "that she's mentally unstable, and they're questioning whether she should have been allowed to work on the show in the first place."

There are five pictures of Spencer and me leaving the restaurant, and I do look a lot like a stalker. One of them was taken just as he pulled his hand away from mine, so I'm reaching after him and have red eyes.

Then I scroll farther down the page and my eye catches on something in the comments at the bottom.

Kz<3lolz552: Spencer Black soooooooo hottttt I <3 him to DEATH.

DeeLuvsTheHalls: Stalk me!

Anon: OMG, Google Gabi Morgan. Looks like being a nutbag runs in the family!

The link goes to the article from the local paper last year about my dad.

Local man "insane with grief" at death of father in supermarket breakdown

CHAPTER 40

A reporter came to the house when only Dad was home. He'd just been discharged from the hospital, and Mom had gone out to get some food. The reporter told Dad he just wanted to present his side of the story, and so Dad talked to him, like he does to absolutely everyone who knocks at our door; we usually have to send Millie out to stop Dad from signing up for some scheme or becoming a Mormon. Dad invited the journalist in for a cup of tea and told him everything. The journalist stole a picture of Grandpa and one of Dad from the night we all went to a sing-along version of *The Sound of Music* and he was dressed as a brown paper package tied up with string. They didn't even explain that when they ran the article, which made people think that he had his breakdown while wearing a cardboard box.

When Millie and I got home from school we could tell

immediately that there was something shady about the man. We shouted at him and chased him out the door. In the article he said that, as well as dealing with his grief, Dad was struggling to control his two rampaging teenage daughters, which must have contributed. It went into lots of detail about him flinging cans of beans around the supermarket, tipping over stalls of flowers, and tearing at his own clothes. And there were interviews with other people—someone in the supermarket who'd been hit by a flying potato speculated on what Dad would have done if he'd had a knife, and a parent from our school said she wasn't surprised because Dad had always been weird.

I told Granny that when sad things happen I let everything build up and pretend I'm fine—just like Dad did. And I told her that I'm worried I'll end up doing something crazy like he did. She said that the thing that annoyed her most about the article was that it made out there were such things as "crazy" and "sane."

"Everyone has something," she said, "and everyone deals with life in different ways. I can't promise you'll always be okay, but I can promise that you will always have people around to help you."

And I will. Unless I break their heart and push them away.

I storm out of the room and walk straight into Spencer in the lobby. He has an armful of flowers and a paper bag and a box of chocolates in his other hand. Up until that point I've been telling myself that the comment could have just been some random person from home who saw the article when it came out. Then I see his face.

"I'm *so* sorry. My agent was asking me about you and I told her your name. I thought it would be some story about a love triangle on set—you, me, and Heidi. I didn't think it would make you out to be crazy."

I can't believe what I'm hearing. "You knew it was coming out?"

"My agent told me yesterday. She said it would up my profile to have a few stories on gossip sites. But I swear I didn't know it was going to be that. It's a stupid article about nothing—no one will even spend two seconds reading it."

"That's not the point, Spencer."

"Come on—most people who read it won't know you and won't care."

"I said it's not the point! You let it happen. I should never have trusted you."

"So you just expect me to trust you, then? Even though you haven't bothered to mention that you went out with someone for three years and only broke up with him two months ago?" His eyes are flashing angrily and his face is red.

"How did you know that?"

"You're not exactly private with what you put up on your Facebook page. And while we're there, you've written a ton of stuff about wanting to stalk people from *The Halls*, so you might want to watch that."

I barge past him and hear him drop everything as I go through the door. It would look all dramatic and like a scene in a film, I think, if the flowers weren't mixed up with bacon.

I walk around forever feeling like I'm going out of my mind. Hours pass, and I even forget all about lunch.

I end up on the bridge over the Thames right next to the London Eye. So I find a bench and sit down. I try calling Mia, but it won't connect. My thumb hovers over Nish's and then Rosie's name, but I haven't spoken to either of them since the picnic.

I know the one person I want to call. But I can't.

So I call Granny.

I'm alone again for a while, and then I feel him sit down beside me.

"Hey."

"Max?"

CHAPTER 41

I swallow. I feel like I've got a rock in my throat again. My eyes hurt.

"Your granny called me."

He puts his arm around me. I only have to move my head a little to the side and it fits in the crook of his shoulder like it always did. He squeezes my arm and stands up, pulling me with him.

"Come on," he says gently, "we're eating."

"I can't at the moment."

"Don't be an idiot. Let's go."

We're in a Chinese buffet, and I go to pick up my fork but get the sick feeling again and put my hand back down. Max already has a forkful of noodles, and he points it at me as he talks.

"I've seen you eat, Gab. You'd usually wolf this down and then start on mine."

I breathe in to try to speak and then stop because I can feel that my voice is going to come out all high and weird.

"What's stopping you?" he says softly.

I swallow again. It hurts. Stupid rock. "Just . . . worries."

Usually words fall out of my mouth before I've had the chance to think about them. But now they're locked in. I meet Max's big brown eyes.

I'm thinking about how the same thoughts go around and around in my head and trap me, and I can't ignore them long enough to do anything normal, like just talk to people. And I'm thinking about how the thoughts are circling my stomach and squeezing it so I can't eat. Or speak.

He's just waiting. That's what he's like—no pressure. He lets me be me and just waits. I take a deep breath.

"I worry that I'll end up losing control like Dad did. And I'll push everyone away."

He looks at me steadily. "You don't have to worry about me. You never will."

I look down at the plate.

"I'll always be around," he continues. "Even when you get bored and run away to London."

I look up then and he's smiling. I grin back, and a couple of hot tears drip over my lip and into my mouth. I've started crying. I never do this. I blink rapidly to try to get rid of them.

"You can always come back and hang out. As friends, or as whatever. Just as us." He hands me a tissue. "But maybe when you're a little less snotty."

As if on cue, I give a large sniff.

"So . . . What's been going on?" he asks.

He wants me to tell him about Spencer, and when I ask if he's sure he wants to know, he takes a deep breath in.

"Hit me. I can take it."

I tell him about how I never know where I am with Spencer, and how at first it was exciting, but at the same time I don't know how much I can be myself.

"Maybe I just need to grow up," I say miserably.

"Please don't," says Max. "I want you to always be the girl who interrupted a wedding by laughing when the priest said 'loin.'"

"Ha, and when he said 'sexual union,' putting tons of emphasis on *sexual*."

"My cousin was so not happy about you laughing at her wedding." Max smiles.

"She should have gone to the justice of the peace, then—they don't say loin or sexual in that one!" I tell him.

Our laughter is interrupted by my phone going off in my bag.

I have fifteen missed calls from Spencer and a text. When I open the message a whole bunch of writing comes up, and it looks like the longest text in the world. While I read it, Max sits there and looks at his plate.

```
So I'll start with sorry. I'm really,
truly sorry. I got caught up in the
whole fame thing and I didn't think.
Now I'm sitting alone (smelling
of bacon and flowers, by the way),
```

realizing that the highlight of my
summer wasn't getting a part in the
show—it was meeting you. You're
ridiculous. And you've made me laugh
pretty much nonstop. And when you care
about someone, you tell them properly.
I left it too late to tell you that I
fell for you the moment I saw you fall
off a train.
You want me to know you, and I don't
yet. But I want to. And I think it
will be an adventure.
If you want to join me, meet me at the
London Eye at 8.
I'll be the dickhead in the suit
holding champagne—how's that for a
finale?
Spencer x

Max looks up.

"Well?"

"He's . . . he's waiting at the London Eye with a glass of
champagne. Like in the show."

Max manages a sort of smile and nods. "He's good."

The bill comes, which breaks the tension for a moment,
and soon we're back outside again. The London Eye looms
in the distance on the other side of the river.

"So, you probably need some time to think," says
Max. "I'll . . . head off. But, you know, if you need
anything . . ."

I want to tell him that I don't want time to think. I want him to talk to me and to not have to think at all. There's a pause when we don't know whether to hug. Then Max puts his arm out to do a fist bump instead. We laugh, and then I grab him and hug him. I cling to him, burying my face in his chest, and then we break apart.

As I watch him walk away, I get a sad pang when I notice he's wearing the hat I got him. I wish I'd gotten him the one he really wanted.

Walking along the bridge, it feels like everyone else is going the other way. They're walking lazily in the after-glow of a hot day, and it seems as though everyone I pass is in a group of friends, chatting and laughing. I thought that's what I'd get from the summer, but it hasn't really turned out like that. Because I've been focused too much on Spencer?

But this is a person I could have adventures with.

I see Spencer in the line for the Eye, wearing a suit and trying to open the champagne bottle while holding the glasses. People keep looking over and pointing at him, maybe wondering whether he's proposing to someone. Or perhaps they've seen his YouTube show.

In the show, Harry was dressed similarly and got into a pod on the Eye, looking at his watch as the music got more dramatic. Then he saw Jen, standing on the grass. She shook her head and the pod moved off, and the credits rolled. And it was such a shock, because you'd seen her running and you really thought she would go to him.

It makes me decide. I do the same. I run.

I get there just in time. He was about to go. I grab the back of his arm, and he turns around. He looks surprised.

"Look, would you come back with me?" I ask him. "I just want someone to be with me and listen to all the crap I say and just hang out."

Max laughs. "Sounds amazing."

CHAPTER 42

Granny has gone out for dinner, so I lead Max over to the ladder to go up to my bedroom. He follows me up without saying anything.

In the bedroom, I get into my pajamas and walk over to the bed. He takes off his T-shirt and then starts undoing his jeans. Then he looks up at me.

"Hey! No peeking—face the wall."

I smile at him and turn around.

My phone lights up in my bag. I told Spencer I would explain in the morning. I don't know if he'll want to see me. I don't know what I'm going to say. I read his reply. It says, Okay.

Max and I slide under the covers and lie side by side, looking up at the ceiling.

"I love you," he says.

"I love you, too."

And I know, whatever kind of love it is, we do love each other.

I don't need to be in his arms to feel that he's there for me. I turn my head to the side, and so does he. And I talk about everything.

CHAPTER 43

It's such a relief to be honest with him. When all the stuff happened with Grandpa dying and with Dad, I just used Max to distract me. I wanted everything to be the same. I went out most nights and spent as little time at home as possible. And everyone was saying how well I was doing—how it was great that I didn't let things get me down. But I felt like I'd turned into a joke. I was doing what everyone expected of me—getting drunk, saying stuff without thinking, getting engaged too young—and they thought that was all I was. I thought everyone was laughing at me and Max behind my back, just like they were laughing at my dad. And I started blaming Max for how I felt people saw us.

"I never thought you'd care about stuff like that," Max says when I tell him.

"Neither did I," I say, my voice getting squeaky and tears

still streaming down my face. I think that because I don't cry very often, when I do, I unleash a flood. Mostly of snot, it seems. "I just wanted to prove to people I could do things on my own and that I wasn't stupid, so I came to London for the internship."

"No one thinks you're stupid, Gabi."

"Your parents do. When they prattle on about you going to college and being a musical genius and how I'm holding you back."

"Well . . . my dad's a dick."

"Yeah, he is."

I feel Max's stomach tensing as he laughs. It's nice to be this close to him again.

"Anyway," he says, "you're the only one out of all of us with the prospect of an actual job. You're Julia's favorite waitress, and that's pretty special—she's fired most of the others."

"But, Max, you should have seen how they were all look-ing at me. They kept telling me I could take the rest of the shift off or take a break. Even when I got things wrong, I didn't get told off."

Max is quiet for a while. Then he moves on the bed and clears his throat. "This summer you've done things on your own. You lived here. Did the internship. Did the hot new TV hunk . . ."

I elbow him sharply in the ribs. "Shut up, you."

"What? Are you embarrassed to be half of a hot new celeb couple?"

"I was embarrassed when I went to a fancy hotel, threw wine at him, and then woke up in the middle of the night and hallucinated a dead bird. But I don't need to worry about that anymore. I'm not so sure we're a hot celeb couple now."

I feel his arm sliding away from me.

"Max . . . ," I warn.

"What?"

"Do *not* do the happy dance!"

Too late.

"Max!" I try to hold down his arms, but I can't stop laughing. Eventually I smack him on the side of the head. "Anyway, what have you been up to—hanging out with Rosie?"

He stops the dance and frowns at me. "Huh? Rosie's going out with my brother."

"WHAT? No!"

"Yeah, they met at this party just after you left. But she was really worried about telling you, I think—because she's been over to our house a ton. It was nice getting to know her a little better; it felt like a link to you."

"I thought you two were having a steamy affair!"

"No steamy affairs for me," he says, "but you should have seen some of their messages!" He stops when he realizes that sounds weird. "Cal lost his phone again, so I said he could use mine."

Once the big stuff's out of the way, we talk for hours. The same silly things we always talked about. Eventually our responses get slower and start making less sense, and at some point we fall asleep.

In the morning he gets ready to go before I wake up. He

knows I'm meeting Spencer. There's a moment before he leaves when we don't know whether to hug or not. Then he grabs me and gives me one of his bear hugs.

"Best friends?" he says.

"Best friends," I reply, my voice all muffled in his hoodie. "Well, equal to—"

"Equal to Mia. I know my place."

Spencer leaves me waiting for about ten minutes in the coffee shop, which is only fair, I suppose.

He sits down, and there's an awkward pause.

"Things got a bit crazy for a while there," I say.

"To put it mildly." He nods.

Then we catch each other's eye and can't help but smile.

"Oh dear," he says.

"Oh dear," I agree.

There's another silence, less awkward this time, and I start to speak.

"I should have told you about Max. But I won't even let myself think about him. He knows me so well, and he saw me struggling through all the stuff with my dad and barely coping. He was the one person who knew what scared me most—that I would have a breakdown like Dad. I liked you being someone who didn't know any of that."

"So you kept me at a distance," he says in a low voice. "You could give me a chance to get to know you as well as he does."

"It's not just Max, it's all of them," I say, finally speaking out loud the thought that came to me when I saw Max sit down next to me on the bench. "All the people who know me and helped me through. My best friends. I need them at the moment, and I need them to know how grateful I am. I know at some point there will be room for a new relationship. But for now, it's them I need."

He nods and gives me a half smile. "Timing, eh?"

"And anyway." I sip my coffee and raise my eyebrow at him. "You're TV's hot new hunk—you'll be beating them off with a stick. Our summer fling will be a distant memory."

"Ha!" he laughs. "Well, I guess that won't be completely unenjoyable."

I meet his gaze. His eyes are sparkly and his eyebrows arch slightly in the middle, like when he first asked me out for coffee. A few images flicker in my head. His body pressed against me. His kisses going down.

I probably shouldn't be thinking about that now. I'm supposed to be all sensible and doing the right thing. I'll think about something else—something totally nonsexual. Like this salt shaker.

Spencer is giving me a funny look. I am staring pretty intensely, to be fair.

"You know," he says, "you are really weird."

"And a stalker," I add.

He nods. "Dodged a bullet, really." There's a pause, and he runs his finger over a scratch on the table. "I won't forget about our summer fling, though."

I smile at him. "Me neither. Best tour guide ever."

I'm standing in the line at the grocery store later. I called Granny to say I was on my way back, and for some reason she said not to come home yet and that it was really important for me to buy a bag of nuts first. Maybe I just have to accept that my entire family is insane.

I tap my thumb on my purse, and then panic shoots through me. I look at my thumb. I've lost the ring again.

Hopefully it just fell off in bed or when I was getting changed. I need to grow bigger fingers. I'll just hide my hand when I go inside, chuck Granny her bag of nuts, and then go straight up to my room.

I see movement in the window as I come back up the path. It looks a little speedy for Granny, but you never know these days. Then when I open the door, I have the shock of my life—they're all there. Granny, Nish, Effy, Rosie, Max, his brother Cal, Han and some of the other girls from school, Millie, Jamie, and . . . Mia!

CHAPTER 44

Mia didn't really hit her head when I knocked her over. She only hit it on Jamie's knee. I'm sure she's fine. I'm certainly not letting her out of this hug anytime soon. She's trying to say something.

"What's that? Did you say, 'I love you, Gabi'?"

I can't believe Granny invited them all over. This is literally the best surprise ever.

"She said, 'We brought cheese,'" says Jamie, towering above us.

I release Mia and walk over to him. "Ugh, you're still on the scene, are you?"

"You'll have to come with us next time," Jamie replies. "Mia kept whining that she had no one to go crazy dancing with. I did try—I wore my best dress, but apparently it wasn't the same."

"Next year, for sure," I say, giving him a friendly punch on the arm.

He frowns and looks at me seriously. "I'm glad you're okay."

"Thanks, Jamie."

"Right," he says, and walks off, no doubt to balance out his moment of being nice with lots of grumpiness.

Standing behind him is Nish.

I walk sheepishly up to her. "Do you hate me?" I say.

"Yeah, that's obviously why I'm at your surprise party," she says, and we both smile.

"I'm really sorry about the picnic. I was awful," I say.

"Don't apologize. We're all awful sometimes," Nish replies.

Next I walk into Rosie and Cal, midkiss.

"Why didn't you tell me, you fool?" I say as Rosie breaks off the kiss and turns bright red.

"I . . . just thought you'd find it really weird, me being at Max's house all the time. I'm sorry!"

"Oh my God, don't say sorry. I was a dick. Anyway, I'll leave you to your smooching and steamy texts." I wink at her, and Rosie turns even redder, if that's possible. I don't say anything to Cal—I'm still wary around Max's family, but he does smile at me. He has to be nice to me now that he's going out with one of my friends. Because if he does anything to hurt her, I will kill him.

After a high-five with Han, I head over to Granny and give her a hug. She knew that the kind of leaving party I needed was one with all the people I'm going back to and have been missing. She always knows these things. Apparently a bag of nuts was the first thing that came into her head when she was trying to think of a way to keep me out of the house. I told her I hope she always says things like that and never becomes normal.

I look around the room at everyone: Mia showing Rosie and Cal pictures from France; Jamie and Max standing awkwardly next to each other and not speaking; Nish and Effy in their own little world. For the first time in months, I feel totally relaxed. There's nothing hiding at the corner of my mind to worry me.

Once Granny's given me some sangria, even though it's only lunchtime, we drink a toast.

"To Grandpa!"

CHAPTER 45

"So, Gabi," Julia says, her arms crossed. "What are we going to do with you?"

"I want to come back. I've had a totally awesome summer. Well, mostly. But Radleigh Castle is what I know. And I'm good at it. And . . . Oooh, Dan's back!"

He gives me a thumbs-up and a grin as he disappears into the kitchen.

"You know he's totally in love now with this Polish girl he met when he was traveling?" I say. "There were about a million photos of them on his Facebook page."

"Lovely," says Julia dryly.

We walk along to the restaurant in silence. Julia picks up the schedule from behind the bar and starts looking through it.

Suzy is polishing glasses and showing off a sparkly engagement ring to one of the other waitresses. I remember with a gulp that I never found Granny's ring. I haven't told anyone and am totally panicking about how I can replace it. Where do you buy old, irreplaceable, priceless rings? I distract myself—as I've been doing every time I think about it—by talking, and I tell Suzy how nice the ring is and how good it is that big Welsh Scott with the beard finally proposed. She thanks me and asks if I'm coming back to Radleigh.

"Yep!" I say. "I mean . . ." I look over at Julia. "Hopefully. I think so . . ."

"We'd love to have you back, Gabi." Julia smiles.

"Thanks so much!" I think I'll hug her, but as I lunge toward her she holds her hand up.

"But! I don't want you to still be here next year."

I stop midlunge. "What?"

"I want you to do something else," Julia says. "You could go to college, or—"

"Do you think I'd get in?"

She looks at me sharply. "If you don't go, then it will be because you've chosen something else. You can if you want to. Or you can do something with this TV experience. Or do the same job you do here—but not here. And if in five years you want to be my wedding planner, then give me a call. But go and have some adventures first."

When I do hug her, Julia looks like she might die of shock.

I walk back along the river into town. My first shift is tomorrow. One more year, and then . . . who knows? I might start looking things up when I get home. I'll get Mom to help me—she always gets overexcited about that sort of thing.

Oh my God, if I took some courses in writing for TV, then all my hours of watching soaps and dramas and reality shows and anything starring attractive people would actually be *research*!

When I'm waiting to cross the road at the edge of town, a car pulls up to the lights. It's Max's mom.

Today is the day he's leaving for college. The backseat is jammed with stuff, with Max's *Jurassic Park* duvet lying across it. Max's mom gives me a sort of smile from the driver's seat, and then Max leans around from the passenger seat and sees me. He points to the shirt he's wearing and grins at me. It's his Barcelona jersey. I never gave it back after we had that argument, but I took it with me when I went to say good-bye to him a few days ago and sneaked it into his bag of clothes.

We're still grinning at each other as the car pulls off.

When I get home, I hear Mom squeal from the kitchen. She comes running over, holding out a little bag.

"*Someone* dropped this off for you!" she says, and winks at me.

"Who?" I say, taking it.

"Now that would be telling," says Mom.

Millie sticks her head over the banister. "It was Max."

Dad walks through the hall on his way upstairs. He narrows his eyes suspiciously and mutters, "Boys."

Inside the bag is a little blue box with a gold clasp—the

one that Granny gave me. Inside the box is the ring, but as I take it out a delicate gold chain comes with it.

Max's note reads:

So you'll stop losing it.
I can't wait to see you next week in Leeds.
M x

Gabi: Best. Weekend. Ever.

Mia: What did you do?

Gabi: I ran down a road in my underwear surrounded by naked men.

Mia: Of course you did. What else?

Gabi: Well.

1. So Max's housemates are all girls—Katya, Rach, Zannah, and Laura. He is very happy about that and kept grinning. I told him that he's not allowed to like any of them until I've checked them all out. I'm not having him go out with anyone terrible. He said he doesn't think he'll go out with anyone for a while. We had a little bit of a moment then and maybe kissed, but only a bit. The housemates seem nice, though. I gave them all cookies to try to make them be my friends. Laura tripped up and fell headfirst into a door when she arrived, so I think she's my favorite.

2. Rach has dyed red hair, so I thought I would see if she would let me call her Mia and dress her up as you. She didn't say no. Or yes. She didn't actually say anything.

3. NUDITY. We went out to the Student Union and they had these drinks called Snakebite Black that were only £1 and didn't taste of alcohol, so I had six. Then we were walking back to the dorms and saw AN ENTIRE RUGBY TEAM running naked down a path. Apparently it was some sort of initiation thing. It was the happiest moment of my life. Then Max said "Don't!" because he knew what I was thinking—how funny would it be if I joined them?? Answer: Very. So I did. There are photos.

4. I almost died on the train home. I felt so ill. I was sitting there rocking and moaning. So when I got into London I went in search of coffee. The coffee stall I found was Taste of Spain—there was one near the university when I was on my internship. And it was the same guy there that I'd met before, this guy named Felix. When I got my coffee I saw he'd written his number on the cup!

5. I got another e-mail alert about Spencer—there's a rumor that he and Heidi are going to star in their own reality show called *Hencer* . . .

So I'm nearly back now and will stop writing because I will soon be talking to you. We have big plans to make for my amazing 18th birthday extravaganza. You had better be waiting for me at the station or there will be trouble. Ooh, actually I'm pulling in now and can see your face. YAAAAY.

Xxxxxxxxxxxxxxxxxxxxxxxxxxx :)

ACKNOWLEDGMENTS

There are many, many people who made writing the difficult second book so much easier. Thank you to all of you!

First, Anne, my agent, for loving Gabi as much as I do.

Everyone at Piccadilly Press, especially Brenda, who made it all possible. Melissa—Best. Editor. Ever—for knowing exactly what I wanted to do with this story and for helping me get there.

Then to all the lovely friend-and-family people who gave me so much support and enthusiasm when *Irresistible* came out. Mum, for equipping every single member of my family with a copy of the book. Dad, for not teasing me too much about my "steamy" status. Edd, for being the person I knew I could e-mail when I needed a pretentious sentence about ancient Greece. Granny and Grandpa, for more things than I could possibly fit on a book page. Ruth and Eloise, joint best cousins ever. Hazel, for cheering me up to no end with chats over rare steak, and a winky face ;). The TWGGS massive: Emily, Han, Laura, Lorna, and Lizzie, for making me laugh through school and ever since. The lads: Claire, Tanya, and Hazel, for hilarious e-mail chains, full of comedy gold. Non, best boss ever. And Tess, Anna, Celia, Nadia, and Ryan, for support, awesomeness, wine-drinking, and humor.

Finally to all the bloggers, writers, and readers who wrote lovely things about book one, particularly Luisa Plaja for the Chicklish review, Siobhan at Bookalicious, and Polly and Amber from my old school TWGGS—it would be really cheesy if I told you just how happy I was to read your words, and we'd all end up feeling a bit awkward, so, you know, THANK YOU.

And you (I wouldn't forget you)—thanks for reading!